The BLOOD Of The SON

"The Father sees no son in the one who spills innocent blood, no matter how loud he kneels"

—Book of Judgment, 1:1

The Blood of the Son

By: Lopez

First Edition—MMXXV

Printed in the United States of America

ISBN: 979-8-9937359-0-0

Cover design by the Author

Interior design by the Author

Published by Veiled Truths Press

www.thelopezbooks.com

For *my parents*—who taught me honor, resilience, and what it truly means to carry a name.

Acknowledgement

Special thanks to Sergeant Baltazar, whose guidance helped ensure the police procedural aspects of this book remained grounded in truth. Your friendship and service have always been deeply respected.

Bellavista

Bellavista was a small suburb just outside of Los Angeles—one of those forgotten cities no one really speaks of. It didn't have a beach, a ball team, or a skyline. Just heat-scarred pavement, liquor stores on every corner, and a city council that hadn't held a clean vote since 1986. The kind of place where graffiti outlived mayors and the only time the news vans showed up was for a shooting or a scandal. Usually both.

City council members were under federal investigation again—fraud, embezzlement, kickbacks from construction contracts that never broke ground. Meanwhile, law enforcement could barely keep the Eastside Malditos and Los Varrio Ghosts from turning the neighborhood into a war zone. The two gangs had their own rules, their own leaders, and their own sense of justice. The only thing they shared was a hatred for each other and a strange respect for one man: Don Rafa.

Just last week, Officer Ortiz—a decent cop by Bellavista standards—was gunned down outside the corner store on Gage and Vernon. Wrong place, wrong time, or maybe just not enough backup. His death was chalked up to "ongoing tensions," the kind of phrase that sounded clean in a press release but meant something real ugly on the streets.

But before the city could wake up, before the engines roared and the sirens howled, one man was already moving. The sun hadn't cracked the skyline yet, but he was there—keys in hand, coffee in a dented thermos, and a slow, heavy walk that said he'd done this a thousand times before.

Don Rafa was opening the shop.

It was 5 a.m. The sun hadn't shown its face yet, and Don Rafa was already fishing out his keys just as Elias Konig pulled up in his silver Mercedes. He parked beneath the old elm tree— the only spot on the property with a working security camera. Whether that was coincidence or calculation, no one ever asked.

"Good morning, Mr. Konig," Rafa said, voice steady, routine.

"Morning, Rafa. How's the family?" Konig replied, like he always did. Same question every day, more habit than heart.

"They're well, Mr. Konig. Thank you for asking." Rafa answered, as he slipped the key into the front door of Konig Kustoms—a shop known in Bellavista for turning trucks, Impalas, and Cutlass Supremes into rolling statements.

The kind of place where paint met pride, and chrome wasn't just a finish—it was a language.

The key turned with a familiar click. The heavy door groaned open, and Rafa stepped inside. The air was thick with the scent of lacquer, rubber, and spent brake cleaner—a cocktail only mechanics and painters could love. It lingered in the cinder block walls like ghost smoke, soaked into every rag and shop coat hanging by the lockers.

Rafa reached for the wall panel and flicked the first switch. Then the next. And the next.

Click. Click. Click.

Each one lit a section of the shop—cold fluorescent tubes stuttering to life like old soldiers being called to attention. In the front window, the neon "OPEN" sign buzzed to life with a faint glitch, the bottom half of the "P" flickering like a nervous eye.

Mr. Konig didn't say much else. He gave a half-wave and climbed the metal stairs to his office above the front lobby—a glass box with a mini fridge, a dusty computer, and a view of the whole shop floor like some kind of throne.

Rafa didn't look up. He didn't need to. He was already moving.

He set his thermos down beside the faded invoice tray, pulled out the orders from the day before, and started lining up the paperwork. Chuy had three tint jobs scheduled—one full wrap, two strip replacements. Manny had a custom audio install on a 1991 Suburban. Rafa mentally built the schedule as he walked, his boots echoing across the smooth concrete floor.

At the back wall, the work board stood tall—a whiteboard crusted at the edges with old marker stains, magnets clinging to faded clipboards. Rafa grabbed a rag, wiped off the last job from yesterday, and started writing fresh:

Bay 1 – Chuy – '95 Tahoe – Rear limo wrap

Bay 2 – Manny – '91 Sub – Full deck, amp, and mids

Bay 3 – Open

He'd fill that last one by lunch. He always did.

Before long, the smell of burnt coffee would fill the break area. The radio would start crackling to life with Chalino or Los Tigres. The shop would wake up—and the city with it.

But for now, Rafa had work to do.

By 8 a.m., the shop had life. The scent of body filler and overspray danced in the air as the sun finally broke over the rooftops of Bellavista. The first to walk in was Chuy, wearing a faded grey Bellavista High School hoodie with the sleeves cut off and a roll of tint tucked under his arm.

"Buenos días, Don Rafa," he said with a respectful nod.

"¿Qué hay en la pizarra hoy?"

Chuy moved with the kind of calm that came from surviving too much. A veterano from Los Varrio Ghosts, he'd walked away from the life when La Sombra Negra started buying loyalty and calling shots. He didn't like the way things changed—less honor, more silence. But Chuy had earned enough respect to walk out in one piece. Now he just kept to the work.

Rafa handed him the clipboard without looking up. "Tahoe en la uno. Full wrap."

Just then, Manny strolled in like he owned the place—Locs sun glasses still on, hoodie halfway zipped, and a SoBe bottle in hand. His gold chain caught the morning light as he threw his backpack down near the lockers.

"What's up, Chuy?" he grinned, pulling off his shades. "Don Rafa—buenos días. Where's your boy at? Just 'cause he's the boss's kid don't mean he can show up whenever he wants."

He let out a chuckle, half-joking, half-jabbing.

Rafa raised an eyebrow, not even pausing as he filed another invoice into the tray.

"No mames, güey. He'll be here soon."

The front bell chimed.

And just like that—Junior walked in.

The shop door creaked open. Junior strolled in, grinning like he owned the joint—not out of arrogance, but because he knew he belonged.

"Hey, Pops! I'm here—al que esperaban." He stretched his arms wide like he was onstage.

Rafa didn't even look up.

"Mijo, stop playing around and get to work. Go help Manny with the Tahoe—y esta vez be sure to use the right heat shrink on the wires, and the 30-amp breaker for the amp. No se te olvide.

Junior gave a lazy salute with the burrito in his hand. "Alright, apá. Mom sent you a burrito de huevos con chorizo. Be sure to eat while it's warm. It's breakfast, not lunch."

Rafa paused, eyes softening for just a second.

"Dile gracias."

Junior placed the foil-wrapped bundle near his dad's thermos, then headed toward the bay, already unwrapping his own as he walked. Chuy nodded at him, silent as always, and Manny gave him a quick head nod from under the open hood.

Junior was the boss's kid—but everyone in the shop knew he'd earned his place one busted knuckle at a time.

Junior moved through the shop like he was part of it—like his footsteps belonged between those bays, marked by oil stains and memory. The others used to call him el hijo del patrón when he first started—mostly with smirks, sometimes with attitude—but that didn't last long.

Because while other kids his age were out chasing girls or hanging at the mall, Junior was crawling under dashboards, stripping wires, taping harnesses, and learning how not to fry a sound system.

He showed up before school, after school, on weekends. If a customer came back because of a rattle or loose trim, he took it personal. That was something he got from his dad—an obsession with detail. The kind where one crooked switch or bad solder joint could ruin a whole install.

And even when Rafa was hard on him—especially when he was hard on him—Junior never pushed back. He understood. Respect wasn't given—it was modeled. And his old man was the blueprint.

If someone needed help, Junior was there. If a job ran late, he stayed. If the sun went down, he was still on his back under a lifted Silverado, heat gun in one hand, zip ties clenched between his teeth.

He was still young, still finding his voice—but in this shop, Junior was one of the real ones. Not because of the blood in his veins, but because of the dirt under his nails.

Junior grabbed a roll of wire loom from the parts bin and walked over to Bay 2, where Manny had already popped the rear panels off the Tahoe. Wires were spilling out like guts, and the sub box was sitting half-wrapped in the corner.

"A huevo, finally decided to show up, huh?" Manny said, reaching for a heat gun. "Bout time the niño del patrón earned his keep."

"Yeah yeah, what you need?" Junior replied, already unboxing the amp.

"First tell me something," Manny grinned. "What's the first thing you look at on a woman—her tits or her ass?"

Junior looked up, deadpan. "Her eyes."

Manny stopped mid-strip, blinked, then burst out laughing. "No mames—her eyes? What are you, fifteen? You ever even seen unas nalgas bien buenas, bro?"

He looked around the shop like he needed a witness. "Chuy! Ven pa'ca—oye lo que dijo el morro. El Junior dice que se fija en los ojos. Este cabrón a de ser virgen, ¿qué no?"

Chuy didn't look up from the back window tint he was laying, but a smirk crept across his face.

"Pinche mamón..." Manny added, chuckling as he crimped the speaker wire. "Whatever, Romeo. Just don't forget the heat wrap this time, lover boy."

Junior shook his head with a grin and kept working. He didn't take the bait. That was the thing about him—the jokes bounced off, but the work never did.

By noon the shop was humming like a well-oiled machine,

Los Tucanes de Tijuana blasted through the old stereo bolted to the wall near Chuy's station, the blown-out speaker still pushing just enough bass to carry the corrido:

"Vivo de tres animales, que quiero como a mi vida..."

The front bay doors were wide open, letting in light and the sound of traffic from Atlantic Blvd. Tools clinked, drills hummed, and the air smelled like a mix of sweat, fiberglass dust, fresh vinyl, and Gatorade. The kind of shop flow you couldn't force—it had to be earned.

Chuy was just about done with the rear tint on the Tahoe. He'd already heat-shrunk the wrap tight, his hands moving in that silent, precise way that only veterans had.

Manny was crouched beside the driver's side door panel, sliding in a pair of Pioneer 6x9 three-way speakers, his drill gun whining between quick jokes about how much better trucks sounded back in the day.

Junior, under the dash, wiring up the head unit, paused. Not because of the work—but because of the wall.

He leaned back on his heels, wire crimpers still in hand, and looked up at the photo-covered wall across from the break area. Dozens of pictures, sun-faded and curling at the corners, lined the pegboard. Each one was a build. A story. A name.

There was the yellow LA LEY promo truck with checkered sides and deep-dish Daytons. The airbrushed Silverado tailgate from '95 with the painted mountains and Palo Alto, Jalisco scrolled across the bottom. The candy red GMC with silver ghost flames and a mural of La Virgen rising from the smoke.

Those weren't just trucks. They were reputation, legacy, work ethic on wheels.

That's when the memory hit.

He was maybe eleven when it happened. Still too small to lift a 15" sub box without tipping over, but already tagging along after school. One night, Rafa was laying down purple pinstripes on a pearl white stepside, using nothing but a brush and a steady hand.

Junior stood by the bay door, watching, quiet.

"Why do you still paint them yourself?" he'd asked.

Rafa didn't look up.

"Because my name rides on it mijo."
Simple. Final. Like truth being spoken into the concrete.

That stuck with Junior. Still did.
He snapped out of the nostalgia.

Looked back down at the dash, his fingertips tracing the wire route behind the head unit. Then he smiled, just slightly, and grabbed the heat wrap.

"Manny, pass me the 30 amp breaker."

"Damn son, so you did listen." Manny smirked, tossing it over.

Junior caught it midair and went back to work.

The shop kept flowing.

And outside, Bellavista kept sleeping on the fact that the realest artistry in the city was happening right here, under everyone's nose. Until a slight rumble broke the rhythm of the shop.

The guys looked up just as a brand-new Silverado rolled in—straight off the lot from the dealership across the street. Shiny silver, untouched paint, fresh blackwalls, the gold Chevy bowtie dead center on the grille. The factory sticker still clung to the windshield, and with the breeze from the open cab, that unmistakable new car scent wafted into the shop like money and gasoline.

The truck idled with authority, before shutting off.

Then the driver's side door opened.

Tico stepped out.

Botas de avestruz, black 501 Levi's, and a cinto piteado with a custom silver belt buckle flashing a bold "T" in 24-karat gold. His shirt? Louie Vuitton silk, the kind that didn't come from the swap meet next door. Gold rings, aviator glasses, a Stetson hat, and that trademark Colgate smile—with a single gold tooth glinting in the sun like a warning and a wink.

Tico was a middleman for La Sombra Negra—a cartel born from shadows, power, and blood. Drug routes, human trafficking, now even the local gangs bent the knee when they came around.

He walked past the "Do Not Enter – Employees Only" sign like it wasn't even there. The smell of expensive cologne followed him like a trail of smoke… and so did the feeling that something dangerous had just walked into the building.

"Buenas tardes, muchachos," Tico said, tipping his sombrero as he passed.

He looked at Manny. Smiled just enough.

And then stepped into the office, where Don Rafa was waiting.

Tico

Tico walked into the lobby, the soles of his ostrich boots tapping slow against the concrete, as Don Rafa looked up from the invoice tray.

He didn't know Tico was coming that day. But he didn't need to. Rafa had been doing this long enough to know—some customers you don't see. You feel them.

"Buenas tardes, Don Rafa," Tico said with a grin, tipping his Stetson as he approached the counter.

"Quiúbole, muchacho. ¿Cómo están las cosas en el rancho?" Rafa replied, steady as always.

There were things Rafa knew—and Tico's business was one of them. Not because it had ever been spoken out loud, but because truth has a smell, and shadows have a way of walking through the door wearing cologne and a gold tooth.

Don Rafa wasn't part of the cartel. Never had been. Never would be.

He was a businessman. A craftsman. A man who treated people with dignity, and in return, everyone—on both sides of the line—respected him like a king.

One time, a well-known ranchera singer even slipped his name into a song during a radio set:

"Y ahí le va un saludo a mi compa Don Rafa, de Konig's Kustoms, en Bellavista, California…"

Rafa never spoke on it. He just nodded when it played on the radio and went back to sorting speaker wire.

In the hallway near the breakroom, Junior heard the voice and stepped up to the edge of the doorway, just far enough to listen. He didn't make a habit of eavesdropping—but when types like Tico came around, his curiosity always won out.

It wasn't just what they said—it was how they moved, what they wore, the cars they pulled up in, the women they brought, and the cash they threw around as if they printed it in their garage.

There was something magnetic about it all—dangerous, maybe. But magnetic nonetheless.

Back in the lobby, Tico leaned casually against the counter and reached into his jacket. He pulled out stacks of twenties, wrapped in thick rubber bands, and set them down with a soft thump.

"Mi jefe wants this truck to be better than any of the others. Candy apple red with scallops and pinstriping. Lowered on 17-inch gold Dayton wires. Testarossa fiberglass body kit. Interior de piel de avestruz. And the best sound system you can fit in that cab."

He slid the stacks across the counter, like they were chips at the poker table.

"Y mire, Don Rafa… pa' que no se raje. Ten grand to get the job started. The rest when I come pick it up."

Rafa didn't blink. He'd seen it before. He lifted the stacks from the counter, opened the cash drawer, put the money away and gave a small nod.

"No problem, Tico. You know we always get it done—and get it done right."

Tico checked his watch.

"Bueno, Don Rafa. My ride's here. I'll see you in a few weeks."

He handed the keys over like they were ceremonial—like he knew the truck was about to become more than just a ride.

Then, just before walking out, he turned on his heel.

"Oh yeah, casi se me olvida... He wants a mural on the tailgate. I'll call you later with the details."

Tico walked back out the way he came.

Junior watched—not directly, but enough for Chuy to notice the way his eyes lingered. The shine, the presence, the scent of danger masked in gold and silk.

A white Mercury Grand Marquis idled next to the Silverado. One driver. One passenger in the front. Tico opened the rear door and slid in without a word. The car pulled away like it had never been there at all.

And just like that, everything returned to normal.

The radio kept playing its string of classic corridos, the kind that carried equal parts nostalgia and warning. The phone rang twice before the shop's landline crackled to life. Mr. Konig's voice drifted down from his office window like a mosquito buzz:

"Are you trying to sell me something? You're not a very good salesman!" and slammed the phone down.

Chuy wiped his hands on a shop rag, looked over at Junior, then walked up and gently pulled him aside. There was a heaviness in his expression—not judgment, just knowing.

Chuy had lived through things—things a young man shouldn't have to know exist. But with that came wisdom, and he'd seen the glint in a young man's eyes enough times to spot the pull.

"Mira, carnal," Chuy said quietly. "I know that lifestyle looks attractive. The rides, the clothes, the women... la feria. But never go chasing it. It brings a life of pain and sorrow, okay? It takes more than it gives."

Junior nodded slowly.

He didn't say anything. But he heard it.

He went back to work without a word, head low, hands steady.

The rest of the day passed without much incident. The Suburban was finished, tested, cleaned, and rolled out with a clean slap on the tailgate and a receipt that still smelled like printer toner.

As the light outside started to dim, Junior and Manny were buttoning up a few loose ends, sweeping up the bays, and putting tools back in their drawers.

"Hey, Pops." Junior called across the shop. "It's 6:30. Time to clock out and go home."

Rafa was still by the front counter, sorting paperwork into neat little piles the way he always did. His reading glasses low on his nose, hands moving slow but precise.

"Sí, mijo. You go ahead. I just have to get these papers in order."

He paused, then added,

"Dile a tu mamita que llegaré más tarde."

Junior grabbed his backpack and nodded.

"Okay, Pops."

He stepped out into the evening, keys in hand. But even as he walked away, he knew the truth.

His father wouldn't get home until after eleven.

Every night it was the same—extra work that wasn't his to do, promises that were never honored, a boss that never once said thank you.

Junior loved working with his father. Loved being in that world with Chuy, Manny, the hum of drills and the smell of vinyl. But this part?

This part he hated the most.

At home, Junior usually ate dinner alone.

His mom would almost always wait for Rafa to get home, no matter how late. But she still cooked for them both—always fresh, always from scratch, and always with more love than words could ever express.

Junior sat at the table, finishing up a plate of chile colorado, arroz, and fresh tortillas. After the last bite, he stood, kissed his mom gently on the forehead, and smiled.

"Gracias, Amá. Estuvo increíble."

She smiled back, but the warmth behind her eyes dimmed a little.

"¿Y tu papá?" she asked, drying her hands on a towel.

Junior shrugged. "You know... siempre lo mismo."
She sighed and leaned against the counter.

"Tu papá trabaja tanto que a veces me preocupa que se me vaya a morir allí en ese taller."

Junior didn't say anything.

"Siempre ha tenido esa ética de trabajo, desde que era niño. Ayudando a tu abuelo en el rancho, allá en el pueblo. Desde que llegó aquí, era de un jale a otro, apenas saliendo adelante."

She turned to face him, her voice softening.

"Ese señor Konig le dio la oportunidad en la tienda. Y con su forma de ser, tu papá hizo tal impresión que lo pusieron de encargado."

"Tu papá es un hombre leal, trabajador... y todo lo que hace, es por nosotros. Para que tú no tengas que romperte el lomo como él."

Junior nodded slowly, then looked away.

He didn't have the heart to tell her what he was really thinking—that maybe Rafa didn't have to suffer like that at all, that maybe there were other ways to provide. Ways Tico lived in broad daylight, ways Chuy had warned him about.

He walked into the living room, flopped onto the couch, and turned on the TV.

His favorite show was already playing, the volume low, the glow of the screen dancing across his face.

But his mind wasn't on the show.

It was on the gold belt buckle, the stack of twenties, and the quiet pain in his mother's voice.

"The wise know the war begins long before the first shot is fired—when silence grows too heavy for men to bear."

—Book of the Forgotten, 4:6

Prieto and Pepe

Days had passed since Tico dropped off the truck, and life at Konig's Kustoms had settled back into its usual rhythm.

The shop buzzed with routine: alarm installs, head units, a suspension lift on an F-250 that rolled in from San Bernardino. Nothing flashy. Nothing cartel. Just work—the kind of work that made the days blur together and the weeks slip by without notice.

Then the front bell chimed, and everything shifted.

Prieto walked in.

Leader of the Eastside Malditos, Prieto was a tall, broad-shouldered moreno mexicano with coal-dark skin, thick arms, and an aura that turned heads the second he entered a room. He didn't wear colors or flash—he didn't have to. His face carried the story. His silence told you everything else.

The Eastside Malditos were born in the late 1970s, when Mexican-American families began moving into Bellavista and white flight cleared the streets overnight. As the city changed, funding vanished. The city council got a taste of government subsidies and never looked back.

Money meant for schools, parks, and public services found its way into the pockets of the mayor, city manager, secretaries, and contractors. The Bellavista PD saw a drop in new hires. Patrol cars went missing. And while the city went quiet on paper, the streets began to talk—in new slang, in graffiti, and in gunfire.

Out of that silence came the Eastside Malditos.

Their rivals? Los Varrio Ghosts—or LVG, now led by Pepe, a young shot-caller who took power after Chuco, the former president, who was gunned down outside a liquor store. It was a territorial hit, carried out by an EM foot soldier with something to prove.

The thing is—that territory didn't belong to either of them.

It was a public park. A bus stop. A market lot.

But both sides laid claim anyway, and when lines were crossed, it wasn't paint that hit the sidewalk.

It was blood.

"Ay, viejón," Prieto said as he stepped into the lobby, grin half-cocked like he owned the block. "Brought you my El Camino—need some wheels and tires."

Rafa glanced up from the counter. "Sure thing, Prieto. What did you have in mind?"

"Was checking out those American Racing Torque Thrust IIs in 17s, with some BFGs."

Junior walked in from the bays, wiping his hands on a rag. "Yeah, those'll look clean on the Elco."

"No problem," Rafa said. "I got the tires in stock. Gotta order the wheels. You can leave the car—we'll get it mounted and balanced when they show up. Wheels should be in mañana."

He scribbled a note on the job sheet.

"Total's gonna be $1,545 with labor."

"Simón. That works. Is cash okay?"

"Always."

Just then, the front door chimed again.

"Aye foo—what the fuck you doing here?" Pepe said as he walked in, Güero flanking him like a shadow.

Prieto didn't flinch. "Chill, ese. I'm just here getting some wheels for my ride."

"I don't give a fuck what you're here for," Pepe snapped, jaw tight.

Prieto took a step forward, his cortez's hitting the floor hard.

"Watch your tone, motherfucker. Who you think you're talking to?"

Behind him, Junior tensed. Chuy looked up from across the bay, eyes narrowing, but didn't move.

There it was—the heat between rivals, old beef bubbling up again. But this time it wasn't just about turf. Everyone in Bellavista knew LVG had shifted in recent years. Pepe's crew moved different now—less street, more structure, more money. And word on the street was that La Sombra Negra was pulling the strings.

They weren't just gangbangers anymore.

They were an operation.

That made them more dangerous.

Before things could escalate, Don Rafa's voice cut in, low and firm like a shot through glass.

"A mí me vale madre lo que hagan en la calle... but in this shop, se tratan con respeto."

Silence hit the room.

Pepe and Prieto stared at each other, then at Don Rafa, whose posture hadn't changed—but whose presence filled the space like a steel beam.

"Dispensa, viejón," Prieto muttered. "Didn't mean no disrespect. I'll be back tomorrow to pick up the Elco."

He turned, gave Junior a slight nod, and walked out.

Pepe stood still for a second longer, then approached the counter.

"Sorry, Don Rafa. Se me fue la honda."

Rafa nodded, but his eyes didn't soften. "This place stays clean, Pepe. You know that."

"Sí, señor. Respeto."

And with that, business continued like nothing had happened.

Chuy was in Bay 1, prepping a sheet of tint for a dusty Toyota Camry. His hands moved slow, steady, squeegeeing soapy water from the film like he'd done it a thousand times. Because he had.

"What's up with your homeboys?" Junior asked, walking over. "Lately they seem a little... ballsy."

Chuy didn't look up. "They ain't my homeboys no more. Not for a long time."

He set the tint against the glass, pressed it into place.

"When the cartel started snatching up street gangs—giving 'em ultimatums like, 'Work for us or catch one between the eyes'— I knew it wasn't for me no more."

He paused, then looked at Junior.

"If I hadn't been an OG, leaving wouldn't have been so easy."

Junior stayed quiet.

Chuy continued, smoothing out a bubble with a firm swipe.

"That life... the code we used to live by? It's gone. Back then it was respect, rules. Maybe throw hands. Maybe check a foo. But now?"

He shook his head.

"Now it's all about slingin' dope, gettin' high off your own supply, taking over blocks that don't belong to no one."

He grabbed the rear film, peeled it from the liner.

"When I was a kid, all I wanted was to be a cop. But life had other plans you know. You try to do what's right, but sometimes to survive, you do what you don't wanna do. For me, that was LVG."

He laid the film on the bench and misted it with water.

"Never killed nobody. Beat a few foos down, yeah. That's how it was. But now?"

He glanced over his shoulder.

"Now the stakes are higher. The money's fatter, but your life? It gets shorter."

He looked Junior in the eyes.

"And in the end, you got nothin' to show for it. You think some mom wants to lose her kid to gang shit? Then she's out there on the nine o'clock news, cryin', 'Mi hijo no era cholo', but the pictures they show say otherwise?"

Chuy tossed his rag in the bucket.

"Hell nah."

He sighed and reached for the rear window tint.

"Just watch yourself, Junior. Your pops loves you. Your moms too. Don't screw it up, güey."

He paused.

"I saw how you looked at Tico the other day."

Junior didn't reply.

Chuy slapped the wet film against the rear glass.

"Now help me with this piece. Ándale."

That night, Don Rafa sat alone in the lobby of Konig's Kustoms, surrounded by stacks of invoices, parts orders, and half-drunk coffee.

He moved with the usual rhythm—check totals, noted customer info, cross-reference the job board—but when Tico's invoice slid across his desk, he paused.

The Silverado was about halfway done.

Tomorrow it would come back from paint—candy apple red with scallops, just like Tico ordered. Then Manny would finish the audio install, fine-tune the EQ, and drop in the custom door panels and ostrich leather seats that were already waiting in the back.

It was a hell of a build.

He leaned back in the chair, bones stiff from another too-long day and stared at the invoice like it might tell him something. Something he already felt but didn't want to say out loud.

The old TV mounted in the corner buzzed softly—channel 34, some late-night talk show playing in the background. At this point, it was just noise. Not conversation. Not comfort.

Just something to fill the silence.

The shop was quiet. Too quiet.

And Rafa's thoughts had gotten too loud.

He couldn't shake the tension from earlier.

There'd always been little pot shots between the gangs, un miradón aquí, un empujón allá—but today?

Today felt different.

There was a shift in the air. The kind of shift you didn't hear—you sensed.

The kind that made men like Rafa nervous. And he didn't rattle easy.

He rubbed his hands together, exhaled slowly, and looked around the lobby—the photos, the builds, the parts catalogs, the worn countertop.

He'd given this place everything.

And tonight, Konig's Kustoms had taken enough of his soul.

He stood, turned off the lights one by one, and grabbed his keys from the hook by the door.

It was time to go home.

"Every bullet carries two graves: one for the fallen, and one for the living who remember."

—Book of the Blood, 7:9

Family

Sunday was family day.

After church, Junior, his amá, and Don Rafa always stopped at La Preferida Carnicería on 5th and Gage. They picked up still-warm bolillos, a pound of carnitas straight out of the copper cazos, a tub of refried beans, and three Mexican Cokes—the kind that still came in glass and tasted like real cane sugar and yesterday's childhood.

Back home, amá sliced open the bolillos, smeared a thin layer of frijoles, dropped in a heap of carnitas, then topped each torta with crimson pickled onions. Steam drifted off the meat, mixing with the scent of fresh bread and lime.

The TV in the living room was tuned to Channel 34—one of Rafa's Sunday staples—until the screen glitched and the program cut out.

—"We interrupt this broadcast for breaking news."

The anchor's voice shook slightly. "A six-year-old child was fatally shot this afternoon at Veterans Park. Witnesses report that two rival gangs confronted each other near the basketball court. After a shouting match, a suspect—described as a Latino male, approximately five-nine—drew a semi-automatic handgun and opened fire. Both groups exchanged shots, and a stray bullet struck the child."

The newsroom graphic flipped to a blurred image of police tape and crying parents.

"Criticism has mounted over the delayed law-enforcement response. Chief Ruiz said, 'We are doing everything in our power to bring those responsible to justice.' Local anti-gun advocates are calling for stricter legislation as firearm-related violence continues to climb across Bellavista."

Rafa set his torta down, jaw locked.

"Apaga eso," he said, voice gravelly. Junior reached for the remote and hit MUTE, but the images kept rolling—yellow tape, flashing lights, a child-size sneaker in the grass.

Rafa rubbed his eyes. "¿Cómo pueden vivir consigo mismos esos animales?"

No one answered. The question wasn't really a question.

Junior looked at his father—saw the tired lines around his eyes, the way his shoulders sagged for a second before he straightened—and found nothing to say. He took another bite of his torta, chased it with a swig of Coke, the bubbles stinging the back of his throat.

Outside, someone lit up a lawn mower. A dog barked down the street. The world moved on.

Just another Sunday afternoon in Bellavista.

The TV returned to its scheduled programming, but the news had left its bitter taste in the room. The light from the screen danced over their half-finished plates, now quiet again except for the faint clink of amá collecting dishes.

Rafa sat still, looking at nothing in particular.

"Mira, Junior... in this life, nothing is guaranteed. Ni la tuya o la mía. All we can do is make the most of it, help thy neighbor... así como el Padre Santiago dijo esta mañana. We help each other, and we pray for one another."

Junior didn't respond right away. He took another sip of Coke, the sting of the sugar and bubbles barely registering.

Then he asked, almost out of nowhere, "Did you ever know someone... like that kid? Someone who got caught up in all this?"

Rafa was quiet.

Then he leaned back in his chair, eyes a little distant.

"Yes."

A beat passed.

"His name was Jórge. Back in 1983. We used to work together laying tile in East L.A. Good man. Not a cholo. He wasn't into gangs. Just worked hard and sent money back to his jefita in Guanajuato."

Rafa's voice tightened, just slightly.

"One night he was walking home from the corner store. It was late. He wasn't even supposed to be there." Rafa took a breath to calm his nerves. "Two blocks from his apartment. The gangs mistook him for someone else — and shot him. Like an animal!"

Junior stared at the table.

"They never even caught the person who pulled the trigger. I remember standing at his funeral, thinking... this can't be how it ends for people like us. Silencio y tierra.."

He took a deep breath, folded his arms.

"That's the day I told myself: I'd work. However long. However hard. So that I could live long enough to have a family. So I could raise you. So that you'd never have to be that kid on the wrong street."

Rafa looked up, eyes locking with his son's.

"I know sometimes it looks like I let people walk all over me. But mijo... sometimes surviving means swallowing your pride. Sometimes staying out of trouble is the real fight."

Junior nodded, slow. Not because he fully understood—but because he knew he was supposed to.

Outside, the sound of a ball bouncing in the street echoed once. Then silence again.

Inside, the only sound was the hum of the fridge and the flicker of the TV.

"A borrowed life rides bright and loud, but its debt is always collected in silence."

—Book of Judgment, 18:4

El Gallo

It had been nearly a month since Tico dropped off the silver Silverado. Now it sat in the lot, transformed—candy apple red, fresh pinstriping, custom ostrich-leather interior, and a booming sound system courtesy of Junior and Manny.

Manny stood behind the wheel, fine-tuning the audio setup.

He used "Baraja de Oro" by Chalino Sánchez to dial in the highs and mids. For the lows, he switched to Banda El Recodo—the deep hits of the bass drum and sousaphone rattled the air like a low warning.

Just then, the familiar white Mercury Grand Marquis rolled into the lot.

Tico stepped out of the passenger side, adjusting the cuffs on his silk shirt. "Órale plebón, ahí te miro al rato," he said to his driver, who gave a nod and drove off without another word.

Tico looked around—slow, relaxed, sharp-eyed—and spotted Manny by the Silverado. He walked over, rested a hand on Manny's shoulder, leaned in, whispered something quick and low, then turned and headed toward the lobby.

Chuy and Junior saw the interaction from the tint bay, but didn't say anything. Whatever it was, it wasn't for them.

"Sale pues, compa," Tico said over his shoulder, disappearing into the lobby.

Manny just went back to tuning the amp, like nothing had happened.

Inside, Rafa was reviewing the work order with him—calm, detailed, professional. Tico stood with a toothpick at the corner of his mouth, a gold ring the size of a coin glinting on his finger.

He didn't speak much. Just nodded as Rafa listed out the customizations—the bodywork, the interior, the audio, the suspension tune.

When Rafa told him the balance—eight grand even—Tico didn't flinch.

He reached behind his waist and pulled out a Bancomer bank pouch, unzipped it, and calmly laid out eight crisp stacks of hundred-dollar bills, each one banded, each one clean.

No questions. No counting.

Just a handshake.

Tico walked back out into the lot. Junior watched from the wash basin, his hands still damp, half-scrubbing a pair of headlight housings but not really paying attention.

There was something about the way Tico moved—that quiet confidence, the kind of presence that said "I don't chase respect—I am respect."

Tico approached Manny again. The truck was pulled forward now, idling in the lot, sunlight gleaming off its fresh clear coat.

They shook hands.

Tico gave him a look—brief, meaningful—and slid into the driver's seat.

Then the music kicked in.

Ramón Ayala blared from the doors and subs, loud enough to
rattle the front windows.

The mural on the tailgate glowed under the light:

A white horse rearing in a green field.

Cows and goats grazing nearby.

A rooster perched on a weathered fence.

Mountains behind it all.

A golden sun rising above.

All hand-airbrushed.

And above it, in elegant script:

"Vida Prestada."

A life borrowed.

A life lived fast.

A life everyone knows about—

but no one talks about.

Tico drove off without a word, bass echoing down the block. The truck turned left at the corner, and just like that, he was gone.

After lunch, Manny was back at it—prepping his tools for a quick install. Nothing major this time. Just a head unit, no amps, no custom fab, a clean sixty-minute job. In and out.

He wiped down his panel popper, checked the wiring harness, then called out without looking up.

"Junior—bring me the black electrical tape and the six-inch zip ties."

Junior, who'd just finished sweeping out Bay 3, nodded and headed toward the supply drawer.

"And not the cheap-ass zip ties either, bro. The good ones— the thick ones that don't snap when you breathe on 'em."

"Yeah, yeah, I got you."

The shop had gone quiet again, the way it always did after a big job cleared out. The music was low. Just enough to keep rhythm. The only real sound was the low hum of an air compressor and the faint buzz of a drill from Chuy's corner.

It was a normal afternoon.

But the kind where normal didn't feel normal anymore.

Junior grabbed the tape and ties, and as he walked back toward Manny, he couldn't help but glance at the empty space in the lot where the red Silverado had been.

Gone now. Just like that.

He handed over the supplies.

"Gracias, morro," Manny said, already sliding under the dash of the old Corolla.

Another day. Another job.

But the memory of Vida Prestada still echoed in the back of Junior's mind like the last note of a song that wouldn't stop ringing.

"Hey, Manny," Junior said, wiping his hands on a rag. "What was it that you and Tico were talking about?"

Manny didn't answer right away. He glanced over at Junior, then cut his eyes across the shop to Chuy, who was on the far side of the bays, replacing a set of taillights on a '93 Civic. The new lenses—Altezza-style, straight from R-One Auto Accessories in Cerritos—flashed under the bay lights like cheap jewelry.

"Nada, güey," Manny finally said. "He was just asking about the sonido, you know… how it works and shit."

Junior gave him a look—a short, skeptical one.

"Orale," he muttered, then turned and walked away, not convinced but not wanting to press it.

He didn't know.

Not yet.

He didn't know that Manny had been slinging dope on the side, outside shop hours, mostly in back alleys and parking lots after car meets. He didn't know that Tico was his connect, the one keeping him laced with small packs, no questions asked, just "do your job and stay quiet."

No one at the shop knew.

Or maybe they pretended not to.

Either way, Manny played it cool—like he always did.

But the truth?

It was already bleeding into the bays.

Junior walked out to the edge of the lot, pretending to stretch, but really, just needing a minute to clear his head. He looked out toward the street—same cracked pavement, same slow cars rolling by, same kids down the block kicking a deflated soccer ball against a chain-link fence.

But nothing felt the same.

Not after the Silverado. Not after that mural. Not after the look Tico gave Manny—the kind of look you didn't give someone unless something else was being handed off.

He ran a hand through his hair, cracked his neck, and glanced back toward the shop. Manny was under the dash again, like nothing had happened. Chuy was still at the Civic, wrapping up the tail light install.

Everything looked normal.

But something felt off.

That was the thing about Bellavista—trouble didn't announce itself. It just rolled up, smiled, paid in cash, and left behind a mural no one would talk about.

Junior walked back inside, the late afternoon sun stretching long shadows across the shop floor. He didn't say anything. Didn't ask any more questions.

But in his gut, he knew—

something had shifted.

"The son sees the father bow, and in that bend of the spine, rebellion is born."

—Book of the Blood, 3:12

This Ain't Burger King

The following day, midmorning, Mr. Konig's voice crackled over the intercom:

"Rafa, can you please see me in my office?"

Everyone heard it.
And every head turned to Junior.

He shrugged, trying to play it cool—but his stomach dropped a little. It wasn't like this never happened, but it was still rare.

Rafa wiped his hands, dusted off his shirt, and headed upstairs. He knocked at the office door. Above it hung a dusty sign that read:

"This ain't Burger King—You can't have it your way."

"Come in," Konig called out.

Konig's office was a museum of ego and old dust.

To the left sat a small conference table nobody ever used, now covered in spray cans, rusted tools, and half-forgotten parts. Along the opposite wall were yellowed newspaper clippings of Konig's father, dating back to the 1950s.

There were always rumors—ties to Mickey Cohen, illegal gambling, extortion—but nothing ever proven. And in those days, L.A. was a different beast. Who cared? Who would talk?

Behind the desk, glossy photos and drag racing trophies lined the wall—snapshots of a golden era when Konig's Kustoms sponsored street racers and dominated the blacktop behind Bellavista High, near the old railroad tracks.

Konig, like Junior, once worked the shop floor under his father's command. He'd eventually taken over before the old man died and kept the business running strong. Even served as mayor of Bellavista for a few years—built Veterans Park, expanded the high school, and pushed through reforms to help local businesses.

He got out just in time, too—right before the new city manager came in, started pocketing public funds like it was his birthright.

"Rafa, have a seat. How's the family?" Konig asked, despite already asking the same thing that morning.

"They're doing well, Mr. Konig, thank you." Rafa sat down. "Junior's been learning a lot from Manny and Chuy. He listens, works hard, doesn't complain."

"Good, good. I'm glad to hear it."

Konig leaned back, cleared his throat. "Listen, Rafa… you've been with me what—since Junior was like, four or five?"

Rafa nodded.

"You've been instrumental in growing this shop. When people come in, they ask for you. They trust you. You know this community."

Rafa felt his chest tighten. This is it, he thought.

He's finally going to offer me a real stake in the business… a raise… something that means I'm more than just a piece of the machine.

Twenty years.

Opening the shop at 5 a.m.

Closing up long after Konig was already home.

He never asked for much.

But today, he thought—maybe.

Konig rubbed his hands together. "So, I've been thinking… I'm going to bring in my nephew as the new General Manager."

He said it like he was offering a glass of water.

"You'll stay on as Manager, of course. A bump in pay. Nothing else changes for you."

He gestured with both hands, like he was smoothing the decision over with air.

Inside, Rafa could feel the fire crawl up his spine. He pictured some pendejo in loafers, fresh out of business school, calling shots on a shop he'd never earned, all because he's your sisters son.

But all Rafa said was:

"I understand, Mr. Konig. No problem."

"You sure, Rafa? Seguro?" Konig asked, in his butchered Spanish.

Rafa stood. "Yes, Mr. Konig."

They shook hands.

Firm, silent.

Rafa left the office, closing the door quietly behind him.

He walked back down to the lobby, to the same counter, the same clipboard, the same invoices and orders that had filled his days for two decades.

He stood there for a moment, eyes fixed on nothing.

Then under his breath, barely above a whisper, he muttered:

"Tantos pinches años..."

He shook his head once.

Then went back to work.

Behind the door leading to the bays, Junior stood frozen, having seen—and heard—everything.

He didn't know every word that was said—but he didn't have to.

Junior walked into the lobby, "¿Qué pasó, apá?", his voice low but sharp.

Rafa exhaled. Forced a small smile.

"Nada, mijo. Todo está bien."

But it wasn't. Junior could see it in his father's face.

In the way his shoulders sagged just a little more than usual.

In the way he wouldn't quite meet his son's eyes.

"¿Cómo que está bien? Te estás matando por ese güey—" Junior's voice rose before he could stop it.

"¡Cálmate!" Rafa snapped, his tone slicing through the air.

The lobby went quiet.

Rafa composed himself, took a breath.

"No digas eso." He looked at his son, finally locking eyes.

"Si no fuera por él… quién sabe dónde estaría. Dónde estaríamos."

The silence that followed said everything that words couldn't.

Junior clenched his jaw, bit down on the frustration, and nodded.

But he didn't believe it.

Not anymore.

He turned and walked out—quick, quiet, hot under the collar.

From the bays, Chuy caught sight of him walking through the lot, past the faded "No Loitering" sign, straight toward the liquor store across the street.

Manny looked up from his work.

"What was that about?"

Chuy didn't take his eyes off the door swinging shut behind Junior.

"Sepa la chingada."

Junior walked into the liquor store, the door chime ringing overhead.

"Hello... Welcome," the clerk said, not even looking up.

Junior didn't answer.

He went straight to the back, opened the cooler, and grabbed a blue Gatorade. Paid in silence. Walked outside.

He leaned against the wall, the sun baking the concrete, the plastic bottle sweating in his hand.

Across the street, Konig's Kustoms sat like it always had. Same façade. Same windows. Same peeling paint near the roofline.

And inside?

His father. Still at work.

Junior stared, jaw tightening.

He thought about all the missed Little League games. The birthdays. The family trips that never happened. The quiet "maybe next time, mijo" that always came instead.

"All because of that fucking shop," he muttered out loud.

If only he'd finished college. Made something of himself. Got a career. A real salary. Something—anything—that could've let his pops walk away from that counter, even once.

But here he was.

Same sweat. Same shop. Same cycle.

He took a long sip of the Gatorade, the sugar and electrolytes doing nothing for the storm in his chest.

He was about to walk back across when his eyes focused on something.

Someone. Then it clicked, clear as day.

"Manny."

"Many men chase power to free their fathers, only to bind them in chains of blood."

—Book of Saints, 11:8

Jaimie's Burgers

Junior made his way back to the shop, but something had shifted.

He walked differently. Worked differently.

Mind sharper. Eyes open. Heart colder.

This wasn't just another day. This was the start of something else.

A determination. A plan.

To get his father away from this shop.

Away from Konig.

Even if it meant stepping into places Rafa never would.

He went back to work.

Installed an alarm system. Mounted and balanced a set of wheels and tires. Everything routine. Everything clean.

But the whole time, Manny was on his mind.

Why did Tico pull him aside?

Why did he keep looking at him?

Twice.

Junior didn't need proof.

Deep down, he already knew.

Manny was into something.

Big or small, didn't matter.

He was Junior's way in.

Near closing time, Chuy was in the lobby with Rafa, going over the job board for the next day.

Junior saw his chance.

He walked over to Manny, kept his voice low. "Hey, Manny… what's up with you and Tico?"

Manny paused.

Looked at him.

"I don't know what you're talking about."

"Come on, bro. No soy pendejo."

Junior leaned in. "I saw how he looked at you—twice. Once when he dropped off the truck, and again when he picked it up. And that little platica in the lot?"

Manny kept his eyes on the floor. "That was nothing, Junior. Just forget about it."

"It didn't look like nothing to me."

Junior glanced toward the lobby—Chuy still with Rafa.

He turned back.

"Aye, foo, listen. I don't like how things are going with my pops.

And if there's something you know—make some extra cash, a way to come up? Help a brother out."

Manny hesitated.

Then—quietly:

"Okay. Meet me tonight. nine p.m. At Jaime's Burgers. We'll talk more then."

He turned slightly, kept his eyes on the bay entrance.

"Now go find something to do before Chuy gets back. And act cool, foo— se te nota en la cara."

Junior nodded and walked off just as Chuy came back into the bays.

Chuy looked at Manny.
Then looked at Junior.

And without a word, thought to himself:

What the fuck just happened?

Jaime's Burgers was more than just a burger joint in Bellavista—it was a testament to the enduring spirit of its founder and the community it served. Established by Jaime, an immigrant from Guadalajara. In the late 1940s, it began as a modest burger stand on the corner of Gage and Winslow Avenues. Over the years, Jaime's dedication transformed it into a beloved 10-booth restaurant, and by the late 1960s, following the Vietnam War, it expanded to accommodate 30 booths.

Tragically, Jaime's only son, Michael, a casualty of the Vietnam War, never had the chance to inherit the family business. Now in his late 70s, Jaime continued to run the establishment, its future uncertain without a successor. Yet, for the community, Jaime's Burgers remained a cherished gathering spot—a place where high school students congregated after classes and on weekends, sharing stories over burgers and fries.

It was here, amid the familiar clatter of dishes and the aroma of grilled patties, that Junior met with Manny. The neon sign flickered above, casting a nostalgic glow, as they sat in a corner booth, the weight of unspoken words hanging between them.

Manny sat across from Junior, working through a basket of fries and sipping from a tall Coke. A double cheeseburger, piled high with everything, sat untouched on the tray.

Junior had nothing but his own Coke.

His fingers tapped the table, his knee bounced under it, his nerves obvious.

He watched Manny's rhythm: bite, chew, sip, smirk.

Finally, Junior couldn't take it.

"Ya basta, güey," he hissed under his breath.

Manny laughed, calm as ever. "Relax, bro. Why so tense? Bájale."

He leaned forward, wiped some salt from his fingertips. "So what's up? What do you want?"

Junior swallowed hard, voice dropping.

"You know... what we talked about at the shop."

He hesitated. "I want my pops out of Konig's. I think... you can help."

Manny popped another fry in his mouth, finally pausing. The cheeseburger still sat there, steaming in its wrapper.

"What exactly do you think I do?" he asked flatly.

Junior shifted in his seat.

"I don't know... It's the way Tico looks at you. It feels like there's more going on. Like... something not exactly legal."

Manny's whole energy changed.

The shop jokester was gone.

Now he looked calculated. Measured. Cold.

He pointed a fry at Junior like a knife.

"Mira," he said, voice steady. "Don't sit there like a pussy and expect me to tell you what I do."

He leaned in closer.

"You say it. Con huevos, cabrón."

Junior's chest rose and fell.

"Alright. I think you're slinging dope on the side."

Manny set the fries down carefully, wiped his hands, and leaned back in the booth—his arm draped along the top of the seat, his face unreadable.

"So you think I sling dope. And you think I can get you in. That right?"

Junior nodded.

Manny stared at him.

"What makes you think you got what it takes?"

"To hustle day and night—working the shop and slinging? To hide that shit from jefe and jefita?"

"What makes you think you can handle it when the shit gets real—when you gotta blast some foo just to see the sun rise the next day?"

He pressed two fingers hard against Junior's forehead, just above the eyes.

No one around noticed. But Junior felt it—like a bullet of truth sliding under his skin.

His hands trembled.

He didn't know if he had it in him.

All he knew was... his options were running out.

Then he said it. Quiet. But clear.

"I don't know if I have what it takes."

He looked up, locking eyes with Manny. "All I know is that I want my pops out of Konig's. You saw that bullshit the other day. My pops has worked his ass off to the bone for that foo. He deserves better."

Manny didn't flinch. Didn't smile. Didn't blink.

But something in his stare shifted—just slightly.

He saw it now.

The fire.

He still wasn't sure Junior had the stomach for what was coming.

But for his pops? That cabrón might just do anything.

There was a weight behind Junior's words that stuck with Manny. Not just love—but something darker underneath. The kind of fire that didn't die when snuffed out. The kind that scorched everything in its path.

Manny didn't know it yet, but if anyone ever touched Don Rafa…

Junior wouldn't just burn bridges.

He'd burn cities.

"The first step into the shadows is never loud—yet it echoes for a lifetime."

—Book of Judgment, 32:1

The Lay of the Land

The next night, full of anticipation and uncertainty, Junior waited in the spot Manny had told him.

The outskirts of Bellavista—the industrial section—sat quiet, hollow, and forgotten.

Old warehouses and assembly plants lined the cracked streets, their windows broken, their loading docks rusted shut. Once alive with the grind of machines and the hum of paychecks, now they stood abandoned, left behind as jobs were shipped to China in the pursuit of cheaper labor and fatter margins.

Years ago, the city had tried to do something here—built a Salvation Army shelter, a last-ditch effort to support the community. But its strict rules—no drugs, no drinking, mandatory sobriety—kept many away.

So the streets became home.

Cardboard boxes lined the alleys.

Shopping carts sat full of aluminum cans and rags.

The shadows moved differently out here.

In the distance, headlights appeared, cutting through the gloom.

A Honda Civic hatchback rolled up—lowered, clean, and loud with purpose.

It was Manny.

The car rested on 16-inch Enkei wheels, wrapped in Falken Azenis performance tires. It was well-known in the import scene—a scene that was exploding in Southern California.

Once dominated by fire-breathing V8's and Detroit muscle, the streets now belonged to JDM builds, turbocharged four-bangers with independent engine management systems, tuned for speed and stealth.

The street races still happened—Compton, San Pedro, Torrance—but the names were changing. The machines were different. The rules were different.

Manny rolled down the window just enough.

"Get in."

No questions.

Junior slid into the passenger seat.
The Civic growled, and they drove off into the night.

Manny and Junior cruised through Bellavista, the hum of the engine, the blow-off valve whistling between shifts, filling the silence as they passed through familiar streets.

For a while, no one said a word.

Then Manny spoke, calm but sharp:

"Look around, Junior. What do you see?"

Junior glanced out the window. "I don't know... high school kids, families, homeless people."

Manny shook his head slowly.

"You know what I see?"

He paused, eyes scanning the sidewalks.

"Customers. Every single last one of them."

"They got a need. I got the product."

Junior turned, stared at Manny—but he wasn't smiling. He wasn't playing.

This wasn't the Manny from the shop.

This was someone else. Someone who saw Bellavista not as a home—but as a market.

Junior looked out again—really looked this time.

The family outside the taquería.

The teenager lighting a cigarette near the bus stop.

The guy in the hoodie walking with a limp, nodding off on his feet.

The old woman pushing a cart.

He'd lived in this city his whole life.

But now… he saw it differently.

He always knew there were addicts, sure.

He'd seen the glass pipes, the bent-over figures, the deals going down if you watched long enough.

But he never imagined it could be everyone.

That the clean-cut guy at the gas station might be picking up.

That the girl with braces and a backpack might be fronting for her older brother.

That Manny—the guy he'd worked beside for years—was part of it.

Not a bystander. Not a witness.

A supplier.

Manny and Junior kept driving, the hum of the engine rolling low beneath streetlights that flickered overhead.

The yellow stripes on the road stretched and blurred through the windshield.

Junior glanced at Manny, but he just kept his eyes forward, focused.

Then, without a word, Manny slowed down, signaled right, and turned into a narrow back alley.

They pulled up to a brick building, its walls tagged with layers of graffiti—some fresh, some faded, all claiming territory.

The roll-up door was cracked halfway, and inside, KRS One played low on a battered stereo system.

Manny shut off the engine.

"Come on. Let's go."

Junior hesitated. "Where are we?"

Manny didn't answer. He just stared at him for a moment— stone-faced.

"Don't worry."

He stepped out, whistled loud:

"¡Abre la cortina, güey!"

The roll-up door creaked and buzzed, rising halfway.

Inside, under a bare bulb and that hip-hop beat, stood Pepe—leader of Los Varrio Ghosts.

He squinted when he saw Junior.

"What's this foo doing here?" he snapped.

"Relax, dick—he's with me." Manny said.

Pepe threw up his hands. "Ah hell nah."

But before he could say more, Manny stepped up, right in his face.

"Hey, pendejo—out on the street, you might be the shot caller… but in here? I'm the big dog."

He pounded his chest once. "Me, motherfucker."

Junior froze.

He couldn't believe what he was seeing.

Manny, the same guy who cracked jokes at the shop, had just punked out a gang leader.

Pepe didn't move.

Didn't say a word.

He just stood there, jaw tight.

Then… he backed off.

Slow. Controlled.

The other LVG homies posted up inside the building didn't say a thing.

They just watched.

Because they all knew—

Manny wasn't just anyone.

He was Tico's soldier.

And nobody fucked with La Sombra Negra.

Manny clapped his hands and raised his voice:

"Hey, listen up."

The warehouse went still.

"Most of you already know—but for those that don't, this is Junior. He works with me and his pops at that fuckin' gringo's shop. He loves his family, and he wants to do right by them."

Manny's eyes scanned the room, locking with each man inside.

"I'm taking him under my wing. Gonna show him the lay of the land.

Understand this—nobody, and I mean nobody, better lay a motherfuckin' hand on him.

You make sure he's protected.

Because if a single hair on his head gets disturbed—you won't just be answering to me… or to Tico.

You'll be getting a visit from Los Cuervos.

¿Entendido?"

Silence.

Then slow nods around the room.

Even Pepe nodded.

He didn't like it.

But he knew his place.

Especially if he valued his life.

It was close to midnight when Manny dropped Junior off at home.

The street was quiet. The Civic idled for a beat before pulling away into the darkness.

Inside the house, Rafa was in the living room, the glow of the TV flickering across his face.

El Show de Platanito played on screen, laugh tracks echoing through the room.

"¿Qué onda, mijo? Where were you?" he asked casually, not turning from the screen.

"Manny me invitó a unos tacos. He wanted to show me some mods he did to his hatchback."

Rafa nodded.

"Okay. Vete a dormir. I'll see you tomorrow at work."

Junior nodded back.

"Buenas noches, apá."

He disappeared down the hallway, into his room.

Rafa stayed on the couch, watching his show.

Not knowing that his son's life
had just changed forever.

"Resentment sown in silence grows into roots no man can cut away."

—Book of Judgment, 35:6

Business as Usual

The following day, it was business as usual—at least on the surface.

Rafa opened the shop, same as always.
Konig came down from the office, sipping his coffee like it was a ritual.

"How's the family, Rafa?" he asked, out of habit more than care.

"They're fine, Mr. Konig. Thank you for asking."

The guys trickled in at their usual times, wiping crust from their eyes, carrying energy drinks and breakfast burritos, and the shop came alive.

By midmorning, the air was filled with the familiar:

The buzz of drills

The thump of corridos on the radio

The banter that usually bounced off the walls

But today… something was off.

"Hey, Junior—check out that jaina across the street," Manny said, smirking.

"Man, she's got some legs."

Junior glanced over.

"Simón."

And went back to work.

No grin. No joke. No reaction. Just flat.

Chuy noticed immediately.

He looked over at both of them.

Manny was bobbing his head, singing along to the radio while prepping some wires and RCA cables. Same old clown.

But Junior? He was at the wire cabinet, quietly pulling spools of 18-gauge red and green wire. No rhythm, no vibe.

Usually, Junior would've fired back with a joke or at least a side comment. But now?

Just Simón.

Something had shifted.

And if Chuy had to put a name to it… it was Manny.

Mid-afternoon, Manny dipped out on a supply run—said he needed solderless terminals, wire loom, and self-tappers. Warehouse was 20 minutes away. Probably longer if he stopped for snacks.

Perfect.

Chuy set down his tools and called out:

"Hey, carnal. Cáile."

Junior walked over, trying to shake off the vibe.

"What's up, bro? Need help with tint again? You getting old, foo."

Chuy wasn't laughing.

He looked him up and down. Eyes narrowed.

"What's up?" Junior asked.

"I don't know. You tell me."

"What do you mean? Everything's fine."

Chuy crossed his arms.

"¿Y por qué la cara larga?"

"You've been dragging your ass all day. What's going on?

Spill it, foo."

Junior held his ground for a second. Then cracked—just a little.

"En serio, everything's good. It's just… the other day, with my pops and Konig…"

He looked down at the floor, then back up.

"A veces me encabrona. But my pops is all chill—like 'everything's fine.'"

Chuy stared at him, hard. He knew there was more.

But he also knew when to press—and when to let something simmer.

After a long pause, he nodded.

"Okay, carnal. But you know I got you, right?"

Junior nodded back.

"Yeah. I know."

They slapped hands.

Patted shoulders.

And went back to work.

Some time later, Junior walked into the lobby, the sound of the vending machine humming faintly in the background. He slid a few coins in, hit the button, and grabbed a cold can of Coke as it dropped.

Rafa was behind the counter, clicking away at the keyboard, placing orders.

Pioneer head units. Alpine 6x9's.

A couple of 12-inch sub boxes for stock.

"Hey, apá. ¿Qué haces?" Junior asked.

"Just filling some stocking orders. We were running low on some stereos and speakers. ¿Y tú?"

Junior popped the tab on the Coke and took a sip.

"Got thirsty."

He stood there for a beat, looking at his father. Then—

"Hey, pops... you ever think about doing something you like? You know... something that's yours?"

Rafa stopped typing.

He looked up, surprised.

Junior had never asked anything like that.

He studied his son's face for a second, then leaned back.

"Mijo... it don't matter if it's mine or not.

I've been working my whole life—desde chamaco, mocoso, en México... hasta ahorita.

What I know is work.

Ponme donde quieras—I work my ass off.

Get shit done.

Just like you should be doing.

Ándale—get back to work."

At that moment, Konig walked down the stairs from his office, dressed like always—pressed slacks, smug smile—his nephew trailing behind him.

"Oh, Junior! Hi!" Konig called out.

"Your dad's always telling me how proud he is of you. Says you're a hard worker. Quick learner. Good to see it. Keep it up."

Junior forced a nod.

"Thank you, Mr. Konig. I uh... better get back to work."

Konig smiled and turned back to Rafa.

Junior walked away, the Coke can still cold in his hand, but something in his chest felt hot.

"Hijo de puta," Junior muttered under his breath.

Behind him, he heard Konig say:

"Rafa, this is Justin. My nephew..."

As Junior disappeared back into the bays, the lobby settled into silence again.

Konig's voice faded behind the door—still talking to Rafa, still name-dropping his nephew like it mattered to anyone but him.

Chuy stood just outside the break room, one hand holding a bottle of water, the other resting against the doorframe.

He'd caught enough.

The look in Junior's eyes. The way his jaw clenched.

That moment of silence between father and son, broken only by Konig's rehearsed compliments.

And then—"Hijo de puta."

Chuy didn't flinch.

He just stood there, watching Junior walk away.

There was a weight in that kid's shoulders now, something new.

Not grief. Not laziness.

Something darker. Focused. Quietly burning.

He'd seen that look before.

In mirrors. In rearview windows. In the faces of homies who didn't make it past twenty.

Junior wasn't going toward LVG.

That was Chuy's road. His mistake.

But La Sombra Negra?

Same ending.

Different road.

Chuy took a long pull from his water bottle. Didn't say a word.

Just watched the shop lights flicker overhead as another day bled into night.

Trial by Fire

A few days had passed since the night at the warehouse.

Since the LVG stared him down, since Konig introduced his smug little nephew.

Things had... simmered.

Even the streets felt quieter than usual.

Manny was in Bay 1, working on a clean Monte Carlo.

Door panel already half off, trim pried gently, methodically.

"Junior, cáile."

Junior wiped his hands on a towel and walked over.

Manny leaned back, motioned with a nod.

Tucked inside the cavity of the car, between layers of metal and adhesive, were wrapped bundles—taped tight, dark in color, stacked neatly.

Junior crouched.

Stared.

He glanced across the shop—Chuy was busy in his own bay, cutting window tint for a Jetta.

Didn't see anything.

"What the fuck, Manny? What is that?"

Manny smirked.

"What do you think it is, foo?"

"Tonight—meet me at the warehouse. This ride'll be there. Pepe and the rest are gonna unload it, prep it for distro.

And you?

You're rolling with me.

Gonna show you the ropes. How to move. How to talk. How to sell."

He paused, grinning now.

"You better be ready...

Tico already knows.

You're in it now, homeboy."

Manny laughed, turned back to the car like it was just another install.

Junior stood up, his heart pounding in his chest.

The butterflies weren't butterflies anymore.

They were knives.

He walked off, tried to focus, to breathe—but his stomach twisted.

He barely made it to the restroom.

Locked the door behind him, lifted the toilet lid—

And threw up.

Everything hit him at once.

What did I get myself into?

Can I really do this?

Do I even have a choice?

Three hard knocks on the door broke the spiral.

"¿¡Ey, güey!? You okay in there?" It was Chuy.

Junior wiped his mouth, steadied his voice.

"Yeah... yeah, I'm fine."
"Probably the tacos from down the street."

A beat of silence.

"Okay. Sale pues."

Chuy walked off.

And Junior leaned his head against the stall wall.
Eyes closed.

Trying not to fall apart.

Junior stayed in the bathroom a while longer.

Long enough to breathe.

Long enough to wipe the sweat off his forehead, rinse his mouth, and look at himself in the mirror.

His reflection looked back—tired, pale, but hardening.

He knew what tonight was.

Not just a ride.

Not just a lesson.

It was a test.

A line in the sand.

A trial by fire.

And once he stepped through that warehouse door again...

There was no coming back.

Junior arrived at the warehouse that night, unsure of what to expect.

The air was cool, heavy with exhaust and something else—anticipation.

He walked up slowly, the sound of activity already spilling out from inside.

Ramon Ayala played loud over an old stereo, corridos bouncing off the concrete walls like a war drum.

Pepe saw him first, standing near the roll-up door, smoking.

"Hey Manny—your boy's here."

Manny looked up from across the space, waved him over.

"Cáile, mira esto."

Junior stepped inside, nerves tight, eyes scanning the scene.

Rows of cars lined the warehouse floor—most of them mid-tier sedans and compacts. Nothing flashy. All low-profile.

Manny motioned toward a Nissan Sentra with the rear seats ripped out and the trunk stripped down to steel.

"These rides get packed with shit in Mexico," he began.

"Then we hire drivers—regular people, family types—to drive them across the border.

Once they're over, they park 'em in a shopping center off the 805. About ten miles north."

Junior nodded slowly, taking it all in.

"Then we send some homeboys down, pick up the cars, bring 'em here.

Some I check back at the shop—your pops and Konig don't know shit."

He pointed to a table in the center of the warehouse—packages being weighed, unwrapped, and sorted by masked dudes wearing gloves.

"Once they're here, we unload, inspect, and take inventory.

Then these vatos break it down—prep it into baggies, ready to sell."

Junior's stomach churned.

The buzzing fluorescent lights above felt too bright.

Manny leaned in closer now—voice low.

"Tonight? You and me are takin' about 5 G's worth.

Gonna hit some spots, sell it, move quick.

The other foos are doing the same."

He pointed to a table stacked with cash counters and shrink wrap.

"By one or two, we all meet back here.

Leave the cash.

A few jainas come through, count it up, bundle it, and it's off to Mexico before sunrise."

Manny paused, looked him dead in the eye.

"You do good tonight?

Tico's gonna want to talk to you himself."

He clapped a hand on Junior's shoulder.

"Ponte trucha. Cops be patrolling heavy—especially this side of town.

But we got some on payroll.

If shit's about to go sideways... we get the call."

Junior nodded, but his jaw was tight.

He knew he wasn't ready—but ready didn't matter anymore.

Lessons From the Streets

Manny and Junior started the night cruising the main boulevard.

"Watcha, north of Atlantic—halfway down the bridge over the freeway—that's ours," Manny said, eyes forward, voice sharp.

"Across that? Eastside Malditos territory. From here all the way into L.A.? We run that. Nobody in our way."

He smirked, like the future was already decided.

"Give it three, four months—EM's either gonna join up or get erased. You know what I mean?"

Junior nodded nervously. His palms were sweaty.

"All day long I got LVG crews posted up—liquor store, corner carnicería, even that little church right here—Padre Ibañez runs it." Manny made the sign of the cross as they passed.

"We got a system. Lookouts for the five-oh... and lookouts for the five-oh's lookouts."

Junior blinked. "Wait—what?"

Manny grinned. "Okay, listen. We're out here slinging dope, right? To not get caught, we got lookouts watching for cops.

The cops got a unit watching the lookouts.

But what they don't know—we got counter-intel. Watching them.

You get me?"

"Uh... yeah. I think so."

Junior's eyes scanned the sidewalks.

He was starting to see the city in layers.

The clean version he'd always known... and the real version Manny lived in.

They passed a 24-hour laundromat. A black-and-white Explorer idled in the lot—cops inside, staring them down.

Junior stiffened.

"Relax, foo," Manny said. "Don't give 'em a reason to stop us."

A few blocks later, they pulled into a brightly lit parking lot next to Tacos Don Julio—Bellavista's best, open 24/7.

"Buenas noches, Don Julio," Manny said at the counter.

"Me da tres de asada y dos de al pastor, porfa."

He looked to Junior.

"You want anything?"

"Yeah, I'll take two asada... and three lengua."

Manny nodded. "También dos Cocas de botella, gracias."

They sat outside under flickering fluorescents and the glowing neon sign:

TACOS DON JULIO.

The night air smelled of carne asada and motor oil.

Cars passed. Homeless walked like ghosts—some mumbling to themselves, others asking for change.

A pair of teenagers approached.

"What's up, Manny? Who's your boy here?" one asked, slapping hands.

"Don't worry about it," Manny said flatly.

"What's up?"

"My bad, just trying to conversate. Looking to get a couple dime bags."

Manny looked at Junior.

"Hey, go to the trunk—grab two baggies. Watch your back. Move quick."

Junior nodded, rushed to the driver's side, popped the trunk.

He grabbed a small backpack, unzipped it, found the baggies.

Closed the trunk and hurried back.

He reached over, ready to hand them to Manny.

"Hey! Pendejo—what are you doing? Sit yo ass down."

Junior froze. Dropped into his seat.

Manny leaned in, his voice low but sharp:

"You never, ever, have the product out like that in plain view.
You reach under the table. Always.
Nobody sees shit."

Junior nodded, rattled.

He reached under the table and passed the baggies as Manny
instructed.

One of the teens chuckled.
"What's up with this foo, Manny?"

Manny didn't blink.

"Shut up and get the fuck outta here. My food's coming and I
don't want your stank-ass breath all over it."

The teens dipped.

Junior sat back, trying to process what just happened.

First sale. First mistake. First lesson.

On-the-job training

For Her

Manny decided Junior had taken in enough for one night and dropped him off at home.

It was just past midnight.

Rafa's truck was in the driveway.

Hood was cold—he'd been home for a while.

Junior stepped inside quietly.

He heard his father's snoring—deep, heavy, the kind that only comes after a long day and a silent worry.

He walked into his room, shut the door gently behind him.

Changed out of his clothes.

Brushed his teeth in the bathroom. Rinsed.

Then he stood there—just staring at himself in the mirror.

No cuts. No bruises.

Just a face that felt unfamiliar.

He turned off the light and went to bed.

The next morning, it almost felt like it had all been a dream.

That whole night—a blur.

The warehouse, the deals, the handoff, the heat in his chest.

It all felt far away now.

Like a different life.

Like it happened to someone else.

He sat on the edge of the bed for a moment.

Gathered himself.

Then went into his normal routine:

Showered. Got dressed. Brushed his teeth. Combed his hair.
Put on his favorite cologne

He looked at himself one more time in the mirror—almost hoping to hide whatever he became last night.

"Buenos días, amá," he said, walking into the kitchen.

His mother was already moving around the stove, preparing breakfast for him—and lunch for Rafa.

"Buenos días, mijito. ¿Cómo amaneciste?"

"Bien, amá. Gracias."

"Ah, qué bueno. Ándale, siéntate. Ya mero está listo tu almuerzo," she said, smiling.

His amá was a simple woman from Mexico.

She met Rafa at el mercado in the city center.

Her family ran a small puesto—vegetables, seasonings, things people always needed.

She was maybe sixteen. Rafa close to eighteen.

They fell in love young. Married young.

And not long after, immigrated to the U.S. like so many— chasing a better life.

They caught rides when they could, paid bus fare when they had it.

And at the border, they paid a coyote to get them across.

They knew the dangers—abductions, thieves, murders.

But they were lucky.

They made it.

Junior sat at the kitchen table watching her move:

Pressing tortillas

Placing them on the comal

Stirring the carne de puerco en chile verde

Checking on the simmering pot of pinto beans

She'd cleaned houses her whole life here.

Met a woman who hired undocumented workers.

That was it—cleaning houses since then.

Junior could see it in her eyes—the tiredness.

But when she looked at him, they always lit up.

"Toma, mijo. ¿Qué quieres de tomar?"

"I'll have some orange juice, amá."

She returned with a tall glass, placed it gently on the table.
Then cradled his face with both hands and said:

"Ay, mi niño precioso."

Junior smiled, but something twisted in his stomach.

As he ate, she packed up Rafa's lunch.
Moving with love, never rushing, never bitter.

And all he could think—over and over—was:

I'm doing this for you, amá.
All of this… is for you.

Right?

"Brotherhood born in fear is no brotherhood at all—it is only the leash before the chain."

—Book of the Saints, 9:17

Balance or Burden

A few months had passed, and Junior was starting to find a rhythm—

a strange balance between the shop, home life, and the streets.

At work, he was still Don Rafa's kid.

At home, he still tried to be the same son.

But out on the street?

He was someone else entirely.

Someone who was starting to make a name for himself.

Junior was a quick study.

He picked up the game fast.

He knew:

Which corners moved the most product

Whose faces to trust

Which ones to keep an eye on

Who was on the payroll—all saved on his burner phone

Manny taught him early:

"If you ever get in a jam—

smash the phone and ditch it. No exceptions."

And Junior never forgot it.

His hustle didn't go unnoticed.

Tico took interest.

Told Manny to give him his own route—his own territory.

Junior was efficient. Clean. Quiet.

A rising star in the world of the underground.

And not everyone likes rising stars.

Junior sat on a bench near a local burger joint, just over the bridge that split Bellavista from EM territory.

He kept his hood low. Eyes up.

A couple of regulars walked up, familiar faces.

"Yo, what's up? What you need?" Junior asked casually.

They did a quick exchange—a few dime bags.

"Party in the warehouse district tonight," one of them said, pocketing the dope.

"You should roll through, Junior—it's gonna be poppin'."

Junior nodded. "Maybe. Let's see how the night goes."

"Aight. Let me know." Slapped hands with Junior and left.

Pepe.

He walked up slow with two LVG soldiers flanking him.

That swagger. That smirk.

"What's up, perro? Busy night?"

Junior didn't flinch.

"Maybe. What's it to you?"

Pepe laughed, turned to his boys.

"Ohh, this vato's got balls!"

He stepped closer, chest puffed.

"You might be Manny's little gopher, but you ain't LVG, homie.

Me and my boys? We can teach you a lesson Manny never will...

Respect, foo."

They started to circle.

Junior could feel the air get heavy—real heavy.

He'd been in scraps before. Junior high. High school. Schoolyard rules. His dad would tell him "No te dejes de nadie."

But this?

This was different.

No rules. No refs. Just ego and tension. Raw and real.

Junior stepped down off the bench—ready to fight or run.

His heart thumped hard in his chest.

Then—

A loud whistle cut through the air.

Manny.

"Hey! What the fuck, Pepe? What did I tell you?
This kid is hands-off. Or do I need to remind you?"

Manny pulled a Glock 17—custom stippling, double undercut frame,

gold slide engraved all around.

One side read in bold:

LA SOMBRA NEGRA

He didn't point it.
He didn't have to.

It wasn't about the gun.
It was about the message.

Pepe looked at the piece.
Then at Manny.
Then at Junior.

He smirked. Backed up.

"Vámonos."

They got in his '64 Impala—painted cherry red, white ragtop—
and drove off slow.
Tires squealed soft as they turned the corner.
Gone.
Junior let out a long breath.
Relief flooded his body.

He looked at Manny—still holding the Glock casually.

At first, Junior used to be afraid of this guy.

Now?

They were almost like brothers.
And Junior trusted him with his life.

Manny chuckled, slung an arm around him.

"You good?"

"Yeah, I'm good."

"You sure? You look like you shit your pants, cabrón."

Junior laughed, eyes still wide.

The danger was real.
But so was the bond.
They walked off down the street, neon lights dancing in puddles behind them.

"Come on," Manny said, "Tico wants to see you."

"Beyond the line where nations meet, kingdoms of blood raise their thrones in shadow."

—Book of Judgment, 48:7

Borderlines

The guys headed out to see Tico.

Manny hopped on the freeway, Civic humming low.

"Where we going?" Junior asked.

Manny just smirked.
"You'll see."

Before Junior knew it, they were on the 5 freeway, cityscape slipping past like smoke.

Off in the distance—fireworks.
Bright pops in the sky above the happiest place on Earth.

At least... that's what the sheep believed.

If only they knew the truth.

The ugly truth.

Junior sat quiet for a while.

Then asked, almost out of nowhere:

"Hey, Manny... would you have done it different?

You know—if you had the chance?"

Manny didn't answer right away.

He drove in silence, eyes locked on the road, gears shifting smooth.

"I don't think about that anymore.

Look at our lives.

It would've had to be a very different life for it to go another way."

He exhaled through his nose.

"I saw what I was dealt, and it was either drugs, gangs, or La Sombra.

I chose the one that gave me the best shot at surviving."

Junior nodded, but didn't speak.

He turned toward the window, watching the lamp posts blur by in streaks of yellow and shadow.

He understood.

Even if their lives weren't identical, he understood.

Junior didn't grow up starving.

His parents worked hard, gave him what they could.

But still…

Konig.

That man lived in his head like a virus.

Junior's fists clenched.

"Fuck that foo."

"What?" Manny asked.

Junior blinked.

He hadn't realized he said it out loud.

"Oh... nothing. Just thinking."

Hours passed.

The city faded. Then the suburbs. Then desert highway.

Eventually... Otay Mesa.

Junior looked up. Confused.

"Yo, where we going?"

Manny grinned.

"T.J., homie. Tu tierra natal."

Junior's face dropped.

"What the fuck?! I don't even have a passport, foo!"

"Don't worry about it," Manny said calmly.

"It's all under control."

He pulled into lane number one at the U.S./Mexico border.

A Mexican National Guard officer stepped up to the window.

Looked inside the Civic.

Then at Manny.

Then at Junior.

A small nod.

"Buen viaje, muchachos."

Manny looked at Junior.

Smiled.

And drove forward—

into Tijuana.

Tijuana was everything you'd expect from a border town—and then some.

The streets were alive, pulsing with chaos.

People weaving through traffic, shouting, laughing, hustling.

Brothels lined both sides of the strip, glowing in red and purple neon.

Drunken gringos stumbled from bar to bar, looking for that love money could buy—

if only for an hour.

But be careful.

That taxi you hail?

Might not take you to your destination.

You could wake up in a makeshift operating room,

drugged out of your mind,

hooked up to an IV,

about to become an unwilling organ donor.

Or worse.

If you're a woman...

Junior didn't even want to finish the thought.

Some of them just disappeared—

found later in an industry no one spoke about,

or worse... found in several plastic bags,

dumped across the desolate outskirts of TJ.

Before long—maybe thirty minutes from downtown TJ— Manny pulled up to a massive gate.

The house was tucked inside what looked like a run-down town, cracked sidewalks, shuttered windows.

But this place?

Fortified.

Ten-foot-high concrete walls wrapped the entire block, topped with decorative wrought iron spikes—beautiful and violent all at once.

At the front gate stood two sentries, one on each side.

They wore plate carriers and carried Norinco AK-47s with discipline, not flash.

No gold chains. No tattoos.

They didn't dress like Tico.

They looked like men built for war—mid-20s, lean, silent, deadly.

Their eyes followed every movement like predators.

Competition was fierce between La Sombra Negra and rival cartels.

All of them scrambling for control of two things:

Drugs.

And people.

And that kind of fight?

It spills blood.

On streets.

In mountains.

Everywhere.

La Sombra Negra controlled most of the territory from the U.S./Mexico border down through Coahuila.

But south of that?

A rival cartel was climbing fast—cutthroat, aggressive, and hungry.

The majority of cocaine shipments came from Colombia, passed through the southern border with Central America.

But the rest?

Flew into northern Mexico.

Straight into La Sombra Negra's hands.

And ever since the death of DEA agent Kiki Camarena in 1985, the U.S. crackdown on cartel operations had intensified.

Surveillance.

Pressure.

Military operations.

It made life harder for everyone in the game.

But when your network is as deep as La Sombra Negra's?

Problems like that are just… inconveniences.

Manny leaned out and pushed a button on a weathered comm panel mounted beside the gate.

A voice crackled through:

"¿Quién?"

"Soy yo, Meño. Vengo a ver a Tico."

A pause.

Then—

"Un momento."

A short silence.

Then the response:

"Entra."

The massive wrought iron gates groaned open, mechanical and slow.

Manny eased the Civic through.

The driveway was lined on both sides by massive willow trees, the bases of each trunk painted white in that familiar Mexican tradition.

The trees hung heavy with age, swaying gently under the night breeze.

About a hundred yards in, the trees cleared—

and that's when Junior saw it.

A mansion.

Massive. Imposing.

The kind you'd expect in Beverly Hills, not here.

The house was Spanish-style:

White stucco walls, terracotta roof tiles, arched doorways, wrought iron details woven through every window, gate, and balcony.

The front path opened into a manicured garden,

centered around a marble fountain with a mermaid sculpture rising from the middle—

water cascading down into crystal-lit ripples.

You could see into the first floor from outside—

an open concept layout, the grand foyer feeding into a massive living room with vaulted ceilings.

Two semicircular staircases rose up from either side, curling toward the second floor—

likely where the private quarters were.

But what really stood out wasn't the luxury.

It was the security.

Armed guards stood at every visible corner—

dressed like the sentries at the gate.

Sharp-eyed. Focused.

Willing to die if ordered to.

And just beyond the trees behind the house?

You could barely make out the tops of guard towers,

peeking through the branches like silent sentinels.

This wasn't a home.

It wasn't a mansion.

It was a fortress.

Fortified not just with concrete and iron—

but with men ready to die for the cartel.

For La Sombra Negra.

Sebastian stepped out from the house, greeting Manny and Junior with a practiced smile.

"Ah, caballeros... bienvenidos al santuario. Adelante—Tico los está esperando."

Sebastian was Tico's finance guy.

Every peso, every dollar, every stack of cash that came through La Sombra Negra's hands—he touched it first.

He was in charge of it:

Counting and cataloging income

Tracking who gets paid and when

Scheduling bribes for mayors, police chiefs, and government suits.

Sebastian was Spanish—born and raised across the Atlantic.

He found himself in Mexico nearly fifteen years ago, caught up in a money-laundering scheme that spiraled out of control.

The kind of scheme that steals from the wrong people.

That kind of mistake?

With La Sombra Negra?

You don't survive it.

Unless...

You prove your worth.

Sebastian didn't beg.

He broke down their own system, showed them holes in their financial armor, and taught them how to hide money in plain sight.

He was good.

Too good to kill.

So instead of skinning him alive, La Sombra Negra put him to work.

And eventually, they sent him to oversee Tico—the cartel's biggest earner.

Manny and Junior followed Sebastian into the house, exchanging a smirk behind his back.

His suit? European cut.

Skin-tight fit, pants above the ankle, no socks, loafers polished like glass.

Junior leaned over, whispered:

"This foo look like he missed the runway and ended up at a safehouse."

They chuckled quietly as they walked.

Through the foyer.

Past the towering ceilings of the living room.

And out the back doors.

If the front of the house was beautiful—

the back was Eden.

Directly ahead: the biggest swimming pool Junior had ever seen, glowing with soft underwater lights.

To the left: horse stables, built in the same Spanish style as the mansion—arched entryways, wrought iron gates, tiled roofs.

Inside those stables?

Stallions.

The kind bred only for the world's elite.

Their seed alone sold for millions.

A row of custom-built Razors sat parked nearby—ready to roam the property.

This wasn't just luxury.

This was old-world empire money, soaked in new-world blood.

Junior was still taking it all in when a voice cut through the air:

"Muchachos, pásenle pa'ca."

To the left—Tico, seated at a long custom wooden patio table, waving them over.

The king was ready.

"Every cross in the earth is a debt unpaid, and kings build their thrones upon them."

—Book of the Blood, 14:6

The King's Table

"Meño, ¿cómo estás, compa? ¿Todo bien?"

"Simón, Tico. Todo al máximo."

"Muy bien," Tico said, a wide smile stretching across his face.

It was warm, casual—like they'd known each other forever.

It unsettled Junior.

He remembered when Tico used to show up at the shop.

Even then, he knew there was something about him.

But this?

This was a whole different level.

"Please, Junior, siéntate."

Tico motioned to the chair across from him.

"Estás en casa."

Junior sat down slowly.

Manny took the seat to his left.

Tico reached forward, opened a polished cedar cigar box, and pulled out a Cohiba.

He grabbed a gold cigar cutter, snipped the end with practiced ease, then brought the cigar to his nose.

He inhaled deeply. Eyes closed.

Like he was breathing in memories.

"You know... I have many vices."

He spoke slow, with rhythm.

"Women... liquor... but my favorite? Cigars. Cuban, of course.

Cohiba. Montecristo. Partagás.

¿No crees?"

Junior didn't know how to respond—just nodded lightly.

Tico picked up a gold-plated torch lighter.

The sharp hiss of the flame filled the space—clean, controlled, unnerving.

He slowly toasted the foot of the cigar, turning it until the tobacco burned white at the edges.

Then he brought it to his lips.

Lit it.

Puffed gently.

Rolled the smoke inside his cheeks.

Held it.

Let it out—slow, precise—smiling as a gold tooth flashed through the haze.

Then he laughed.

Looked at Manny.

"Míralo. Casi se caga los pantalones."

He pointed the unlit side of the cigar toward Junior.

Manny smiled quietly, like he'd seen this act before.

Tico had been living this life for so long…

You could see it in his eyes—he didn't just survive death… he walked with it.

There was a hollowness behind his stare.

At some point, after you've done the unthinkable and seen the worst of what men can do...

What's left to fear?

Nothing.

Tico leaned in.

"Tell me... what vices do you have, muchacho?"

His English was broken—but his meaning was crystal clear.

Junior froze.

His thoughts spiraled.

He couldn't speak.

Couldn't think.

"Calma, calma. ¡Rosa!"

A young woman appeared instantly at Tico's side.

"Bring our young friend a shot of tequila.

Manny, ¿quieres algo?"

"Un Tecate. Bien helada."

"Simón, carnal. Rosa, ¡ándale! ¿Qué esperas?"

She nodded and rushed off.

Tico leaned back, puffed again.

"Tonight, my friend... we get to know each other better."

Junior just nodded, stiff and silent.

His throat was dry.

Tico and Manny laughed.

And the smoke curled upward.

After they'd finished their drinks, Tico stood up, brushing the ash from his cigar off his shirt.

"Come, let's take a ride around the property."

They headed toward a line of parked Razors, the lifted off-road vehicles built for speed and terrain.

Out of nowhere, two bodyguards appeared—armed, alert, ready.

Tico, Manny, and Junior climbed into one.

The guards took the other.

Tico fired up the Razor. The engine growled to life.

"Here. Put these on."

He handed Junior a pair of ear protectors—with built-in voice-activated radios.

"These things are loud. Easier to talk with these."

Manny already had his on—he knew the drill.

"¿Listos? Vámonos."

Tico slammed the gas.

The Razor spun, kicked up dirt, and launched forward like a shot.

They flew past the stables—the horses rearing and whining at the noise.

Floodlights cut across the acres of land, even as the first signs of sunrise began bleeding into the horizon.

Junior's adrenaline was spiked.

He felt no fatigue from the hours already spent in Tijuana or the long drive before.

This was surreal.

The wind in his face.

The power of the machine.

The world of the powerful.

Tico's voice came through the headset, steady and cold:

"Ever since I was a young boy, growing up in Sonora...

I felt like I was meant to be somebody.

Not a cop. Not a politician.

No. Something... important."

Junior nodded silently, listening.

"When my father was killed,

La Sombra Negra gave me the opportunity to avenge his death.

¿Y sabes qué hice?"

Junior didn't answer—he couldn't.

Tico continued.

"Not only did I find the man who took my father's life...

I found his family.

His daughter. His only son.

The wife he loved."

"All tied up—right there in the stable.

This was before it was mine.

Back when La Sombra Negra took over this land."

Manny sat in the back, silent.

He had heard this story before.

Only once.

"I told the man,

'You took the most important person in my life…

Now you'll tell me who matters most in yours.'

And I would spare the rest."

"I asked him several times.

Which one would he save?

Wife? Daughter? Son?

Maybe, even himself."

Tico slowed the Razor and came to a stop.

They were near a small, cleared field.

The second Razor pulled up behind them.

Everyone got out.

They walked a short distance until four white-painted wooden crosses emerged from the shadows of the trees.

Silent. Crude. Final.

Tico stood still, looking at them.

"Let's just say...
he didn't exactly give me an answer."

Junior stared, eyes wide.

Horror hit him like cold air.

He turned to Manny—
Manny just shrugged.

This was the cost of power.
This was the code.

"Come on," Tico said, already walking back toward the Razor.
"Let's head back to the house."
They climbed back in.
The sun was rising behind them,
casting long shadows from the crosses across the field.

Every Little Thing

Back at the house, Manny and Junior said their goodbyes.

They headed back toward the States—same way they came.

No hassle.

No questions.

No request for documentation.

Just a simple head nod at the checkpoint,

and they were back on California soil.

La Sombra had eyes on both sides of the fence.

The drive home was quiet.

Junior stared out the window,

Tico's story playing on a loop in his head.

The white crosses.

The calm in his voice.

The certainty.

He could almost see it.

That moment.

Tico standing over them…

The choices. The screams. The silence after.

It made Junior shiver.

He blinked hard.

Tried to shake the image loose.

But finally—

he had to ask.

"What was that all about?"

Manny glanced over.

"You seriously don't know?"

Junior gave him a look—part innocent, part disturbed.

Manny sighed, hands on the wheel.

"He was sending a message, bro.

If you don't fuck with him, his money, or his rep...

you won't end up the fifth cross in that field."

He looked over again.

"Listen to what I tell you, and you'll be alright."

They rode in silence for a few beats.

Then Manny popped open the Alpine faceplate, slid in a Bob Marley CD, and hit play.

The speakers filled the cabin with steel drums and harmony.

" Don't worry… about a t'ing…

'Cause every little t'ing… is gonna be alright… "

Manny sang along, shoulder rolling to the beat.

Junior looked at him sideways.

"No seas mamón, güey."

They both cracked up.

Laughed hard.

Let the tension breathe out through joy.

Two vatos in a car,

trying to find some normal

in a world where normal doesn't exist.

By the time they pulled into Konig's Kustoms, the laughter had faded.

"Buenos días, Don Rafa," Manny said, already rushing to the bays.

Chuy was there, tools laid out, prepping a vinyl wrap on a Dodge Ram—a promo job for a local radio station.

"Buenos días, apá…" Junior murmured.

Rafa didn't look up. "Buenos días."

The silence hit harder than any lecture.

Not because of what Junior had done—Rafa didn't know that yet.

But because he hadn't come home. Hadn't said a word.

As the day dragged on and the heat crept in,

three pops rang out in the distance.

Sharp. Clean. Loud.

The guys looked at each other.

They didn't need to ask.

In Bellavista, knowing the sound of gunfire was as natural as breathing.

They almost went back to work.

Almost.

Until—

"MANNY! MANNY—HELP!"

Güero came stumbling through the parking lot,

white tee soaked red, holding his abdomen.

Blood spilled between his fingers,

dripping down his Dickies, splashing onto the pavement like
red oil.

"H-he…lp me… f-fooo…"

Manny ran to him.

Caught him by the shoulders.

"Hey foo, you can't be here!"

"He…lp mmm…eeee…"

Güero dropped to his knees.

Hard.

Breathing shallow. Eyes rolling.

"Fuck! Fuck! Fuck!"

Manny pulled out his phone, fingers shaking but fast.

"Pepe! Get to Konig's—NOW, motherfucker!

Güero's been clipped! I don't know, just get here—NOW!"

Seconds later—

Pepe's '64 Impala came flying around the corner, tires screaming.

He jumped out, eyes wide.

"¡VERGA!"

He knelt beside Güero.

"Get this motherfucker back to the warehouse—call the doc!

NOW, perro! MOVE!"

Another homeboy jumped out the back.

Together they threw Güero into the car like dead weight.

Sirens echoed faintly in the distance.

The Impala peeled off.

Tires squealed.

Smoke in the air.

Blood on the concrete.

Chuy, Rafa, and Junior just stood there.

Frozen.

Breath held. Minds racing.

From upstairs, Konig's footsteps thundered,

his nephew close behind.

Down the steps. Into the shop. Eyes wide. Confused.

"What the hell's going on?"

No one answered.

Manny calmly walked over to the sink.

Turned on the water.

He rinsed Güero's blood off his hands, the red swirling down
the drain like it was nothing.

They all just stood there, looking at each other.

What the hell just happened?

As they all stood there in disbelief, Manny broke the silence.

"I gotta go."

Konig snapped his head toward him, confused.

"Where the hell are you going?"

Manny didn't answer.

Just stared for a moment.

Rafa looked at him, same question on his face.

No words. Just concern.

Chuy stood with his arms crossed.

He didn't ask.

He didn't have to.

He already knew.

And Junior—he tried to play dumb.

Tried to lead off like he didn't know what was going on.

But he did.

And with Chuy's eyes locked on him?

He knew Chuy suspected it too.

Manny turned.

Walked fast.

Jumped into his Civic.

The engine roared to life.

That turbo spooled with a high-pitched scream,

and then he was gone.

Tires screeched. Smoke rolled.

He was headed to the warehouse.

Shit just got real.

Code 5

Earlier that day, Detective Benavidez sat in his department's morning briefing, arms crossed, already half checked out.

Sergeant White was up front, rattling off updates:

"We've got three new missing persons cases, four stolen vehicles, and the homeless encampment behind La Michoacana is back—owner says they're blocking his deliveries and scaring off customers…"

None of it was Benavidez's concern.

He wasn't patrol anymore.

He wasn't chasing shoplifters or writing parking violations.

He was a tenured detective—twenty-plus years deep.

And he'd earned that seat.

What most people didn't know was that Benavidez used to work at Konig's.

Fresh out of high school, before the badge, before the badge number,

he was just a kid running wire, tinting windows, installing stereos at Konig's Kustoms.

Before that?

He was in the Explorer program—a soft launch into law enforcement where teens learned discipline, rank, how to take orders, and when to break them.

By 17, he got bored of playing Boy Scout.

But the calling?

It was already inside him.

When he turned 20, he got sponsored to the police academy by none other than the Chief of Bellavista PD.

He'd made that strong an impression during his Explorer days.

When the academy papers were signed, Benavidez walked into Konig's shop, shook his hand, thanked him for everything—and never looked back.

He didn't just want a job.

He wanted answers.

He wanted leverage.

He wanted to know what people hid in the dark and why they were willing to kill for it.

"Come on, Sarge," Benavidez said with a smirk during the meeting.

"Let's wrap this up. I got real work to do."

Laughter echoed across the room.

"Thanks to Detective Benavidez's outburst," Sergeant White deadpanned,

"you all owe twenty bucks to the Fallen Officer Memorial Fund."

"Gee, thanks Benavidez," one of the rookies muttered, shaking his head.

Benavidez grinned.

"Alright, alright," White said. "Briefing's over. Last thing—fill out your 180s correctly this time. You're missing key info and I'm not your babysitter."

The patrol units peeled off, heading to their cruisers.

The detectives?

They went upstairs—back to their desks, their phones, their whiteboards full of bad names with red string pinned across.

And Benavidez?

He sipped cold coffee from a chipped mug...

and waited for the phone to ring.

"All units, 246 reported near Konig's Kustoms. Suspects fled in a grey Chevy Caprice. Partial plate reads Adam-Henry-Niner. Time of call: eleven forty-eight."

Benavidez heard dispatch crackle through his radio.

To him, it was just another day in Bellavista.

"BV Sam 4, en route. Responding Code 3."

"BV 12, Code 3, backing." Multiple units responded code 3, lights and siren.

The perimeter went up fast.

Within minutes of the initial call, units were blocking both ends of Winslow and the alley behind Konig's Kustoms.

Yellow tape fluttered in the heat, stretched tight across fences and curbs.

No sign of Güero.

No body.

Just blood. A lot of it.

Officers canvassed nearby businesses, pedestrians, even a few transients tucked behind the corner liquor store.

No witnesses.

Nobody saw a thing.

Bellavista's favorite phrase.

An hour ticked by.

The officer in charge, a steady hand named Officer Navarro, finally called it in.

"Command, this is BV-12 on scene.

Requesting detective response—possible 187, possible gang tie-in. No victim recovered. Witnesses uncooperative. Recommend DS unit."

There was a pause.

Then the voice of the Watch Commander cut through the static:

"Copy that BV-12.

Standby.

BV-DS—respond to possible 187 at Konig's Kustoms. Repeat: BV-DS, respond."

Detective Benavidez was halfway through a cold tamal and a lukewarm coffee when the call crackled through.

He looked up from his desk.

"Shit."

He grabbed his notepad, his badge, and the pair of wraparound shades hanging on his coat hook.

"Let's see what the hell they stepped in now."

He keyed up his mic.

"BV-DS, copy. En route to Konig's. ETA five."

Back at the scene, the officers had already chalked, photographed, and pulled shell casings from the asphalt.

Two 9mm's. One .380.

Classic Bellavista signature.

Rafa and Chuy stood outside the bay, arms folded, quiet.

Junior pretended to sweep.

Konig and his nephew hadn't been seen since the tape went up.

And when Benavidez showed up?

The real questions were finally going to get asked.

Benavidez rolled up in his unmarked Ford Taurus.

One of the patrol officers at the perimeter lifted the yellow tape, gave him a nod, and let the cruiser through.

He parked a short distance from the blood-stained concrete—right where the original crime scene had gone up.

Officer Navarro was already waiting near the edge of the scene.

"What's up, Navarro. What you got?" Benavidez asked, pulling a small notepad from his back pocket.

Benavidez wasn't like the other detectives.

No suit. No shiny shoes. No tie strangling him at the throat.

He didn't need any of that.

His work spoke for him.

He stood there taking notes, slow and methodical—black Chuck Taylors, faded 501's, and a gray Dickies work shirt catching the mid-afternoon sun.

Both arms sleeved in tattoos.

Thick mustache.

Ray-Ban shades.

All grit. No bullshit.

Navarro started running him through the basics—

shots fired, no victim on scene, massive blood loss, shell casings collected, witnesses all blind.

Benavidez listened.

Didn't interrupt.

Didn't react.

Just wrote.

He looked down at the asphalt—

a thin trail of blood curved away from the primary site, heading toward Konig's Kustoms.

"Hey Navarro... you guys catch this?"

Navarro nodded, tired.

"Yeah. Morales traced it back toward the shop.

Said nobody inside saw anything."

He threw up his arms in protest.

"Same story from everyone. Same Bellavista silence."

Benavidez stared across the lot at the shop.

Konig's.

The old stomping grounds.

He exhaled hard through his nose.

Set his hands on his hips.

Lowered his head.

"Shit."

Benavidez made his way toward Konig's Kustoms.

It had been years since he stepped foot inside.

The place still looked the same—

run-down, rusted edges,

like a piece of history stuck in a time loop.

He walked the perimeter slow, boots crunching loose gravel, until he turned the corner and spotted Chuy and Junior standing just outside one of the bays.

"What's up, Chuy? Been a while since I've seen you on the streets."

"Detective," Chuy said, nodding.

Benavidez's eyes drifted to Junior.

He already knew who he was.

But still—

"Who's this?"

"Rafael Jr., sir."

"Orale... so you're Don Rafa's kid?"

Junior nodded.

Benavidez looked down at the blood splatter in the lot, then back up at the two men.

"I see some blood out here. Anybody catch anything?

Maybe the cameras picked it up?"

"Only camera that works is the one out front," Junior answered.

Benavidez hummed.

Not surprised.

"How about it, Chuy? Anything?"

"I know you ain't banging no more.

Pepe swears by it.

You don't owe them anything."

Junior turned to Chuy, eyes searching him.

Chuy stayed still. Measured.

"I don't know anything," he said flat.

"And even if I did?

I ain't telling you. Or any of you chavalas."

Benavidez smirked.

"Oh, muy chingón.

That's alright, porque sabes qué?"

He leaned in just enough to make Junior shift his weight.

"I'll find out. One way or another."

Then turned back to Junior.

"And if the EM boys did this?

Somebody's gonna want payback.

And I don't see Manny anywhere…"

He let that sit.

Looked at Chuy.

Then back at Junior.

"If either of you remember anything… call me."

He slid a business card onto the hood of a Monte Carlo and
walked back toward the perimeter.

Officer Navarro was waiting.

"Anything?"
Benavidez didn't stop walking.

"Nah. But they know."

He scanned the scene—

casings on the ground,

burned rubber still fresh,

a trail of blood like breadcrumbs.

"You know... Manny wasn't here."

Navarro nodded.

"I'll put out a BOLO on his Civic."

Benavidez reached his cruiser.

Opened the door, slid in, and over the radio he heard.

"BV Sam 4 to dispatch. Put a BOLO out on a late model blue Honda Civic.. Person of interest. Last seen near Konig's Kustoms, approximately thirteen-hundred hours."

Dispatch echoed back:

"Attention all units. Be on the lookout for a—"

The radio trailed off.

And without knowing it…

Junior had just stepped into the crosshairs of Detective Benavidez.

And into the center of a storm Bellavista wouldn't soon forget.

"In the house of blood, loyalty is measured not in words but in silence kept and bodies buried."

—Book of Judgment, 61:4

The Warehouse

The warehouse smelled like blood, gun oil, and Pine-Sol.

Junior pulled up slow.

The metal roll-up door was already half open, a soft red glow leaking out from a busted exit sign inside.

He parked in the back—just like Manny told him.

No music.

No engines revving.

Just quiet.

Too quiet.

He stepped through the opening and paused.

Inside, Güero lay sprawled across two plastic folding tables pushed together—shirt cut open, bandages soaked red.

An IV hung from a car jack.

Duct tape held the line steady.

Standing over him was a man in a yellowed lab coat, tattooed fingers working quickly, face half-covered by a surgical mask and sweat.

The Doc.

Manny stood nearby, pacing. Phone to his ear.

"Simón, compa. No, he's still breathing. Yeah… yeah. The Doc says he'll make it."

He looked over at Junior, gave a quick nod, then turned his back.

"Orale. I'll let them know… You sure?"

He paused, listening.

"Alright. I'll take care of it. Myself."

He ended the call, slid the burner into his back pocket, and walked toward Junior.

"He's stable, for now," Manny said, nodding toward Güero.

"Doc says it missed anything vital. Clean through the meat. He'll pull through."

Junior looked at the man hunched over Güero.

"Who is that?"

Manny leaned in low.

"They call him El Carnicero.

Real name? No idea. Salvadorian. Used to be a surgeon, till he messed up some bigshot's kid down there. Fled here under some fake papers.

Tico found him patching up homeless dudes in East L.A. and said—'You work for us now.'"

Junior just stared.

This was another level.

No hospitals. No paperwork.

Just needles, gauze, and silence.

Manny lit a cigarette, blew smoke toward the high beams overhead.

"Tico gave me the green light."

Junior turned.

"For what?"

"To handle it. Personally."

Junior raised an eyebrow.

"No backup?"

Manny grinned—dry, humorless.

"This isn't some movie. No need for theatrics.

We know who did it. And Tico said make it disappear—quiet and final. That's it."

Junior nodded slowly, trying to understand the rules of a game that was starting to bury him alive.

Güero groaned.

The Doc tapped him lightly on the cheek, checked his pulse again, then went back to work.

Outside, a diesel engine rumbled by.

The streets of Bellavista moved on.

Inside, a war was being planned in whispers.

"Hey," Junior said, low enough for only Manny to hear.

"Benavidez showed up at the shop after you bounced."

Manny didn't say anything—just kept flicking the ash off his cigarette like it was nothing.

"Chuy and I didn't tell him anything, but… he's not dumb. He thinks you're involved."

Junior leaned in, voice tense.

"And I heard something else—after you left, I was walking past the lobby, and I overheard Konig talking to my pops…"

Manny looked over, finally curious.

"He said, and I quote:

'If you see him again, tell him to get his shit and get the fuck out of my shop.'"

Still… nothing.

Manny just took another slow drag off the cigarette, blew the smoke toward the rafters, and shrugged.

"Fuck it.

I didn't like that place anyway."

Junior blinked. He expected more.

Some anger, regret, anything.

But Manny?

He'd already cut the cord.

That shop was his past.

This warehouse?

This was his world now.

Manny flicked the cigarette onto the floor, stepped on it, and clapped his hands once.

"Alright, everybody—caiganle."

He waved the others over to the workbench—two LVG bangers and one young dude Junior didn't recognize, maybe 19.

The Doc looked up from Güero and wiped his hands on a towel, watching but not moving closer.

Junior hung back, but close enough to hear.

"Listen up," Manny said, lowering his voice.

"Tico gave the word. We hit back—surgical, clean, no loose ends."

He looked each one of them in the eye.

"No more fuckups. No more shootouts in public.

If someone asks, we don't know shit.

Not even our own names."

Everyone nodded.

Except Junior.

He was still trying to figure out when the ground disappeared beneath his feet.

"Manny, I'ma bounce," Junior said, rubbing the back of his neck.

"This shit's a little thick for me right now."

Manny didn't argue. Didn't flinch.

"I get it. Go home. Rest."

He paused—then looked Junior dead in the eyes.

"But tomorrow... I need you right here."

That look—

It wasn't casual.

It was command.

Junior nodded, kept it short.

"Simón."

He walked out the same way he came—

back through the roll-up door, into the silence of the night.

Manny turned back without missing a beat.

Snapped back into motion, giving orders, tightening the ship.

From across the room, Pepe watched.

Eyes cold. Calculating.

He tracked Junior's exit.

Then shifted his gaze back to Manny—

long and lingering.

"The house you leave in rage becomes the altar you'll one day mourn."

—Book of the Saints, 13:2

The Light in the Livingroom

Junior got home late again—close to 1 a.m.

His dad's truck was in the driveway.

The dim living room light was on.

"Shit," he muttered under his breath.

That could only mean one thing.

It took him back—years back—

To when he was sixteen, coming home after 3 a.m., drunk off cheap beer and adrenaline.

The porch light was off, but the living room glowed like an interrogation room.

There sat Rafa, in his recliner.

His mother on the couch beside him, clutching a rosary.

"¿Dónde estabas?" his father asked.

"¿Y por qué llegas tan tarde?"

The belt came off fast.

No time for lies.

His mother pleaded from the side, voice trembling:

"¡No lo pegues! Rafa—¡no!"

But Rafa didn't stop—

Not until Junior stumbled down the hall, eyes swollen, ribs aching.

He remembered lying in bed, staring at the ceiling through watery eyes.

And then, the sound of sobs.

His father—in the same living room—

Standing alone.

Breathing heavy.

Tears falling.

That night never got talked about again.

But it left a scar deeper than the belt ever could.

Now, all these years later, that same light was on.

Junior stood at the door, keys in his hand, pulse in his throat.

He stepped in.

There was his father—again in the recliner.

Arms crossed, eyes already on him.

TV flickering in the background.

"¿Dónde andabas?" Rafa asked, voice calm but low.

Junior didn't answer at first.

He kicked off his shoes, walked to the kitchen, grabbed a glass of water.

Drank slow.

"I was with Manny," he finally said.

Rafa didn't say anything.

Didn't need to.

Junior could feel the heat of his father's disappointment.

"¿Y por qué andabas con ese güey? ¿En qué estás metido, Rafael?"

Junior didn't answer right away.

"Nothing, pops. He just needed some help."

"Needed help? What does that mean, 'needed some help'?"

Junior shrugged, unsure how to even explain.

"¿Que no miraste que la policía lo anda buscando? What is it, Junior? Tell me what is going on."

"Pops… the less you know, the better."

"¿Qué chingados quiere decir eso?"

"You wanna know? Huh!? You really wanna know?"

"Sí, mijo. Tell me. I want to help you."

"How, Pops? How? All you do is bust your ass at work, you come home tired. I only see you at the shop—we don't do shit together! You never saw me play baseball or basketball. That fucking shop's more important than me or mom!"

Junior's voice grew louder. His mother rushed in, hands trembling.

"Mijo, por favor… es tu papá…"

"No. Fuck that! He wanted to know—well now he's gonna hear it!"

He was yelling now. Tears streaked down his cheeks, his breath ragged, nose flaring, veins pulsing in his neck.

"I got tired of watching you waste away at that place. Konig don't give a shit about you. You're just another Mexican he could use and toss. Yeah—I was with Manny. I went to him to help get you out."

Rafa stood frozen. He never imagined this—never knew his son carried all this.

But like this?

Gangs?

He looked at Junior—really looked—and didn't see his boy anymore. He saw a man he didn't recognize.

With quiet rage in his throat, Rafa's lips curled.

"Te me largas de mi casa."

"…What?" Junior asked, confused.

"¡Que te me largas de esta casa! I didn't come to this country to sacrifice everything. All those years, working like a god damn animal—just to have cholo as a son!"

He pointed to his wife.

"¿Y tu pobre madre, qué? ¿Así le das las gracias? ¡Imbécil, ándale—lárgate!"

Junior stared into his father's eyes.

What he saw wasn't anger—it was disappointment deep in the bones.

His mother collapsed to the floor, crying uncontrollably.

Junior went to his room.

Packed a small backpack.

Crossed himself.

Grabbed his rosary.

When he came back, his father was stone still in his recliner.

His mother, broken on the floor.

He helped her up, kissed her forehead gently, and placed her on the couch.

"Discúlpame, amá. Te quiero mucho."

He turned to the door.

Paused.

Looked back at his father.

Words were there—somewhere—but they didn't come.

His throat closed around them.

So he turned again, stepped outside, and quietly closed the door behind him.

Gone.

Junior drove around for a while before he pulled into the kind of motel where names didn't matter. Just cash, and silence.

"Need a room," he said, sliding forty bucks across the counter.

The clerk barely looked up. His eyes were pale, unreadable. "Three-twelve. Up and right." The key clattered on the chipped counter. Junior grabbed it and walked out into the heat. The air buzzed—electric lights humming, insects thick in the glow. A bulb flickered overhead. Shadows twitched under the stairs. He climbed slowly, each step dragging like a chain. His dad's voice echoed in his skull—"What are you mixed up in, mijo?" Then his mom's face. Broken. Smeared with tears. Her hands shaking. He didn't know what hurt worse: the shame, or knowing he'd do it all again.

He closed the door behind him, the lock clicking like the sound of a decision made too long ago.

The air inside was stale—like old sweat, bleach, and the kind of secrets that crawl into the walls and never leave. He tossed his backpack on the bed and sat down heavy beside it. The mattress creaked like it didn't want to hold the weight of what he carried.

Junior sat there in silence. The hum of the air conditioner. A siren way off in the distance. A car backfiring, or maybe a gunshot. Out here, who could tell the difference?

He opened the drawer next to the bed. No Bible. Just a bent spoon and a torn piece of cloth.

Figures.

His phone buzzed. A burner. Just a number. No name.

"Mañana. nine sharp. Warehouse."

He stared at the screen until it dimmed. Then tossed the phone on the table, laid back, and stared at the water-stained ceiling. He tried to blink the sting out of his eyes. But the truth was already burning.

He missed his mom. He hated his dad.

He loved them both.

And now… he belonged to something else.

"Each crow that perches in silence knows the storm it waits for will be fed with men."

—Book of the Forgotten, 15:9

Retribution

Day One – Retaliation

The air felt heavy on Esperanza Avenue that night, like the whole block was holding its breath. Around midnight, a blacked-out Civic crept to a stop in front of Velasquez Auto, its windows just cracked enough for the barrel of an Uzi to slide through. The gunfire ripped through the silence—quick bursts chewing up the roll-up gate, shattering glass, ricocheting off oil drums inside. When the dust settled, the only thing hit was the shop itself. Nobody hurt. But the message? Loud and clear.

Junior was still awake when the call came through. He sat on the edge of his motel bed, phone glowing in the dark, staring at the text: "Velasquez got sprayed. They ain't playing." He tossed the phone aside, rubbed his face with both hands. He hated this feeling—being sidelined, watching the storm from behind the glass.

Day Two – Drive-by Warning

The next afternoon, the sun was high, baking the sidewalks in Bellavista. A silver Impala with EM plates rolled past a known LVG gathering spot on Amador. The windows were down. No music, no talking. Just four heads turning in perfect sync to stare down the young soldiers posted up out front.

No shots were fired, but the look was worse. Intent. Deliberate. One of them—skinny, tatted up—made a throat-slitting gesture as the car rolled by.

Junior was across the street in an alley, watching it all go down, his heart pounding. He held the pistol in his hoodie pocket, grip slick with sweat. He didn't pull it. Just watched. And hated himself a little for that.

Day Three – Missing

They called him Smiley. Everyone did. Short dude, always grinning, even when nothing was funny. He ran small-time errands for EM—deliveries, stash checks, keeping eyes on the street. On the third day, he didn't show up for work at the tire shop.

At first, no one thought much of it. But by sunset, someone found him in a dumpster behind the Bellavista Swap Meet. Hogtied. Bruised. Two fingernails missing. But breathing.

The word spread fast. No one had to say who did it. Everyone knew.

Day Four – Tag Wars

Art became war.

Walls that had once proudly screamed "EM por vida" were now painted over in black. A skull with crow wings spread across the old taqueria's brick wall. "LVG or lay low" scrawled in thick silver marker beneath it.

Tagging crews moved like ghosts, hitting spots in the dead of night. One kid got caught trying to spray over an Eastside mural and got pistol-whipped in the middle of Atlantic Avenue.

By morning, the wall had changed again: just the silhouette of a raven painted with dripping red eyes.

Junior drove through the city like it was a museum of threats. He noticed the fear in people's eyes. Doors locked earlier. Shops closed sooner. The corner kids stopped hanging out.

Day Five – Funeral

There was no priest. No hymns. Just a quiet group of Eastside boys standing outside the Virgen del Valle chapel. A closed casket rested on the concrete steps. Nobody dared ask who was inside—everyone already knew.

Junior stayed in his car across the street, watching. He recognized the faces. Ghosts of a gang that once laughed too loud and walked too proud. Now, they just stood there. Eyes red. Hands in pockets. Waiting for nothing.

Down the block, a lowrider passed slowly, its bass low and steady, thumping like a heartbeat. LVG plates. A reminder.

That night, the streetlights flickered more than usual. Junior stared out the motel window. The queen bed behind him sat untouched. He hadn't slept in two nights. He thought about Manny. About his last words before heading out. About the weight in his gut that hadn't left since.

Day Six – Stray Shots

Two AM. A shootout on Elm near the old rail tracks. Nobody knew who started it. Just that two guys were hit—one from each side. Paramedics came. So did the cops. But by the time they showed up, both bodies were gone.

Residents ducked under beds. Babies cried. Dogs barked nonstop. One old lady called in a noise complaint and was told, "Ma'am, just stay inside."

That morning, the city woke up angry. Tired. Scared.

Day Seven – Static

It wasn't quiet. Not really. The whole city buzzed with static. Like everyone was tuned to the wrong frequency.

A corner boy ran out of gas near Alameda and got jumped for wearing the wrong colors. A school janitor found a pistol under the bleachers. A taco truck owner closed shop for the week—said he had a feeling.

Even the radio DJs started cutting their night shows short. Less music. More silence. More listeners tuning into the streets instead.

By week's end, Bellavista felt like a shaken bottle of soda. No explosions—yet. But everyone knew it was coming.

And in the motel, Junior finally laid back on the bed, gun on the table, one eye on the door. He whispered to no one in particular, "This ain't the life we wanted. But it's the one we got."

Outside, a crow cawed from a telephone line, and the city waited.

*"The crow does not kill in haste; it waits, patient,
until the traitor stains himself."*

—Book of the Blood, 16:10

The Hit

The streets had quieted down.

After weeks of chaos, Bellavista felt... numb. The sirens weren't as loud. The news cycle had slowed. And though Detective Benavidez hadn't gotten any closer to stopping the bloodshed, he took small comfort in the calm.

A lull was better than war.

He cruised slowly down Atlantic, headlights washing over shuttered storefronts and blinking crosswalks. As he passed Jaime's Burgers, something caught his eye—Manny, posted up outside with a few of his LVG boys, laughing, eating, elbowing each other like old friends at a backyard carne asada.

Benavidez slowed just enough.

Manny looked up.

Their eyes locked—a long, cold stare.

No words. Just knowing.

Then the cruiser moved on, taillights glowing red as it disappeared into the night.

Back at the table, Manny shook his head and chuckled.

"Ese vato stays pressed," he said, stuffing a fry in his mouth.

Pepe sat across from him, leaning back, arms draped over the bench, half-smiling at whatever dumb story Manny was telling. The rest of the crew laughed, wrappers crinkled, soda lids popped, the low thump of a nearby car stereo underscoring the night.

Then—

Flash.

A glint caught the corner of Pepe's eye.

Something shiny.

Something raised.

A barrel.

A figure had approached from behind—quiet, fast, deliberate.

Pepe saw it.

He opened his mouth to say something—

But didn't.

For a split second, he held back.

Just watched.

And then—

BANG.

The flash lit the table.

The sound cracked through the block like a firework wrapped in metal.

Manny's eyes went wide, then blank.

His body twitched once and slumped forward, face-first into his plate. The ketchup mixed with blood. His drink spilled off the table, ice scattering across the pavement like marbles.

Chaos.

The crew jumped to their feet. One guy dove. Another fumbled for his piece. A third froze, eyes locked on the back of Manny's head, where the exit wound bloomed red like a shattered rose.

The shooter sprinted toward the street.

A primer-gray Cutlass idled there, rear door already open.

"¡Vámonos, güey!" someone yelled from inside the car.

The shooter dove in, and the car peeled out, tires screeching, backfiring once as it sped down the block.

One of the LVG boys managed to fire off two shots—wild, rushed, useless.

Then… silence.

Just ringing ears and the smell of gunpowder and grilled onions.

Pepe didn't move.

He sat there, bits of Manny's blood still dripping from his cheek.

No panic.

No rage.

Just stillness.

Satisfaction.

He looked down at Manny's lifeless body—slumped, heavy, head turned just enough to show one open eye—and said nothing.

He didn't have to.

Sirens wailed somewhere down Atlantic, still a few blocks away.

Pepe finally stood, wiped the last of Manny's blood from his cheek with a napkin, and looked at the shaken LVG soldiers around him.

"Load him in the car," he said flatly.

They hesitated.

"Ahora."

Two of them lifted Manny's dead weight and carried him to a waiting Tahoe. Someone scooped up the scattered shells and kicked the toppled tray under a table. By the time the first patrol unit rounded the corner, Jaime's patio looked almost normal—except for a dark slick that crept toward the gutter.

A few hours later at the warehouse, everyone had gathered.

The crew crowded around folding tables under harsh fluorescents, the smell of gun oil and stale fries mixing with frantic whispers. Manny's body lay zipped in a contractor bag near the office door, waiting for Doc and whatever discreet hole he'd arrange.

Pepe raised his chin, trying to look larger than he felt.

"Listen up. Manny's gone—so I'm stepping in. Business continues. We double up on corners, keep the tax flowing, and—"

A heavy silence answered him.

No cheers. No nods. Just wary eyes.

In the back, Flaco—skinny, eagle-tattooed, one of Manny's most loyal soldiers—folded his arms.

"I saw you, homie," he muttered. "You froze up when that vato came up behind him. Didn't even give a warning."

Pepe's gaze snapped over. "Watch your mouth."

But the seed was planted. Eyes shifted. Murmurs spread.

Flaco slipped outside, thumbed open a prepaid burner, and scrolled to the only international number he kept.

Tico.

"Habla."

"It's Flaco. Manny's dead. And… there's something off about Pepe."

"Explícame."

"He saw the shooter, jefe. Didn't do shit."

A pause. Long enough to feel like a verdict.

"Entendido. Mantente quieto. Voy para allá."

Twenty four hours Later — midnight at the warehouse.

Two black Suburbans and a matte-gray armored Land Cruiser rolled up without headlights. Engines low, windows dark. The warehouse door slid open before anyone could knock— LVG soldiers had been told to expect a "supply drop."

Instead, Tico stepped out first: sharp suit, gold-tooth grin, the air around him humming like a live wire.

Behind him moved Los Cuervos Negros—four men in matching dark guayaberas, twin gold Colts holstered cross-draw, a crow's feather tattooed on their right hand. Shadows given shape.

Pepe hurried forward, forcing a smile. "Tico, qué milagro—"

Tico raised his hand. The room went silent. The air had shifted.

The Reckoning

Tico dismissed the room with a wave of his hand.

"Todos váyanse. Menos tú, Pepe."

The crew shuffled out in silence, no one daring to look back. Los Cuervos stood at the entrance like shadows with a heartbeat. The warehouse door slammed shut behind them.

Pepe stood still. He didn't speak. He didn't move. He just watched Tico stroll across the floor like he owned the air in the room—which he did.

"Conference room," Tico said without looking at him.

Inside, the lights buzzed low. Tico took his time, rolling up the sleeves of his silk shirt like he was about to work on a car—or carve one apart.

"Alguien me dijo," he began, voice soft but full of something deadly,

"que al momento que mataron a mi mano derecha… tú pudiste haberlo prevenido. Pero no lo intentaste."

Pepe's eyes widened. "No, Tico—no es así. That's not what—"

"CÁLLATE."

Tico didn't raise his voice. But the silence that followed felt like a blade pressed to the neck.

"A mí no me digas lo que pasó o no pasó."

He circled the table slowly, each step deliberate.

"Loyalty," he said, fingers tapping lightly on the wood. "¿Qué es la lealtad? Some say it's having someone's back, no matter what. Others… they're loyal out of fear. Because they know… that when that line gets crossed—"

He paused, placing a firm hand on Pepe's shoulder,

"—uno paga, carnal."

Pepe sat stiff, barely breathing.

Tico moved closer, pressing a finger to Pepe's temple.

"So tell me… ¿A quién le eres leal, Pepe? Porque para mí, se ve como que tú solo eres leal a ti mismo."

Pepe's voice cracked. "Tico, I swear—I didn't see that vato coming. It happened so fast…"

"¿Tan rápido," Tico said with mock curiosity, "que ni un paso podías dar? Ni una pinche palabra podías gritar?"

He leaned in close. "You were sitting. Comfortably. As if… you were expecting it."

Pepe's face drained. His lips moved, but nothing came out.

Tico stepped back and adjusted his rolled sleeves.

"Pues," he said calmly, "imagino que no tienes nada de qué preocuparte."

He looked him dead in the eye.

"Porque después de esta noche… yo me encargo de todo."

"Tico—wait. Por favor—espera—PLEASE—"

Tears ran down Pepe's face. Desperation spilled in every syllable.

But Tico was already walking out.

Outside the conference room, he gave a small nod.

Two of Los Cuervos moved in silently, closing the door behind them.

A silver Jeep Cherokee pulled into the loading bay. El Carnicero stepped out, gloves on, surgical mask already in place. In the back—gallons of sulfuric acid. Quiet. Clean.

Inside, muffled screams rose. Then… nothing.

Tico climbed into his Land Cruiser and drove off into the night.

No music.

Just the sound of justice being settled, old-world style.

And now, Bellavista was about to drown in feathers and blood.

Los Cuervos

Day One

They came without warning.

No speeches. No threats. No phone calls.

Just silence.

In the early hours, Bellavista woke to screams muffled by duct tape and the rattle of chains against metal fences. On Esperanza, a chop shop burned from the inside out—three bodies charred and curled beneath hood hinges, feathers smoldering in their throats.

No one called it in.

Everyone saw it.

By noon, a taco stand on Soto never opened. The owners—a brother and sister rumored to launder bills for Eastside—were found hogtied inside their walk-in fridge, plastic bags over their heads, rosaries tangled in their fingers. One had bit down so hard on the crow feather it broke a tooth.

EM soldiers started going dark. Phones rang once, maybe twice, and went to voicemail.

By nightfall, the scent of bleach and blood drifted through alleyways like perfume for the damned.

Day Two

Word spread like cancer.

The Cuervos were back.

Nobody said it out loud, but people knew—this wasn't a street war. This was housecleaning.

A garage behind a tire shop turned into a kill room. Plastic-lined walls, a single chair, a blood trail that led nowhere. They found a body in the L.A. River later that day—no ID, no eyes, hands missing, but the mouth packed with feathers like stuffing in a doll.

An EM stash house got hit that evening. No gunfight. No sirens. Just six men butchered like cattle. The neighbors claimed they heard music playing—something old, like a ballad. But no one could say from where.

At dusk, someone hung a pair of boots from the powerlines near Saint Ignatius High.

Size 11.

Black.

Still laced.

By the third night, only fools stayed out past ten.

Except for one.

His name was Tito—young, sharp-tongued, barely old enough to buy a beer. He'd been running with EM for two years. Mostly look-out work. Bag drops. Sometimes tagging over LVG spots just for laughs.

Tonight, he was posted near a liquor store off Soto, nervous but fronting hard.

He hadn't heard from his set in 36 hours.

When the black SUV rolled up slow, Tito reached for the piece tucked in his waistband—

—but never got the chance to draw.

Two shadows stepped out—twin silhouettes in black guayaberas, matching gold pistols glinting beneath the streetlights. A third figure emerged behind them—silent, larger, face hidden behind a red bandana and crow feather rosary.

They didn't run.

Didn't raise their voices.

Didn't rush.

Just walked up like they already owned the block.

One of them leaned in close, calm as confession, voice soaked in finality.

"Ustedes pensaban que estas calles eran suyas," he said softly.

"Pero se equivocaron. Estas calles pertenecen a La Sombra Negra…

y ustedes, pendejos, mataron al mero mero de nuestro patrón.

Y por esas razones, los vamos a mandar al infierno."

Tito dropped to his knees.

"Por favor… no fui yo. I wasn't even there, I swear—"

A boot slammed into his ribs.

He coughed, spit blood, tried to crawl. Another Cuervo grabbed him by the back of his hoodie and dragged him like trash behind the liquor store.

They didn't shoot him.

That would've been mercy.

Instead, they zip-tied his hands, taped his mouth, and pulled out tools that didn't belong in street fights—pliers, a blowtorch, a blade that looked handmade.

He thrashed. Screamed into the night.

Tears mixed with snot and blood.

But as the pain broke through every layer of bravado, only one word made it past the gag—muffled, pathetic, repeated like a prayer:

"…Mamá… mamá… mamá…"

One of the Cuervos paused for half a second.

Then kept going.

By the time the screaming stopped, there was nothing left but a hollow husk of a boy who thought he had time.

They stuffed a black crow feather deep into what remained of his throat and propped him up against the dumpster. A single candle was lit beneath his feet, flickering in the early morning breeze.

A message.

Final. Absolute. Unmistakable.

By sunrise, no one said EM ran Bellavista.

Not anymore.

The Press & Pressure

"Good evening, Bellavista. This is Claudia Ramirez with Channel 34. We begin tonight with developing details in what officials are calling an escalating gang conflict with suspected ties to a Mexican cartel."

Footage flickered across TV screens in living rooms, taquerías, and liquor store counters across the city—grainy shots of yellow tape, flashing lights, and the kind of red that doesn't come from neon signs.

"The Eastside Malditos, a gang rooted in Bellavista's working-class neighborhoods, appears to be at war with a shadowy organization law enforcement believes is tied to a powerful cartel from northern Mexico. While authorities haven't named the cartel, insiders suggest the group known as La Sombra Negra may be behind recent acts of violence."

Cut to Detective Benavidez—standing before a sea of microphones, sunglasses off, sleeves rolled, that tired cop look carved into his face like stone.

"Detective Benavidez, is this officially being treated as cartel violence?"

He gave a measured pause, one hand on his hip, the other holding his notepad.

"At this time, we're not confirming affiliations. What we do know is that multiple bodies have dropped in less than forty-eight hours. This city's bleeding, and it's not by accident."

"Any suspects?"

Benavidez glanced off-camera, jaw tight.

"We're working leads. Right now, our priority is preventing retaliation."

The clip cut back to Claudia in the studio.

"A reminder to our viewers—Veterans Park remains closed tonight after police activity connected to ongoing gang violence. Officials have not released further details, but our sources confirm this is the fifth confirmed incident in under a week."

The news faded into a car insurance commercial.

But across Bellavista, the message had already sunk in.

There was a war on.

And the rules had changed.

After the press cleared out and the mics were packed up, Benavidez lingered. Sunglasses in hand, the weight of too many funerals hanging behind his eyes.

Detective Márquez stepped beside him.

"That's five bodies in seven days," she said. "We can't keep holding pressers while the streets bleed out."

Benavidez didn't respond right away. His eyes were fixed on the skyline—on something no one else could see.

"We need to make a move before the feds step in," he said finally. "They don't care about who started it. They'll sweep up everyone."

"So who do we lean on now?" Márquez asked. "Manny's gone."

Benavidez exhaled through his nose.

"Then we go to Junior."

Benavidez slipped on his sunglasses. "Come on, let's go pay him a visit."

The old LVG warehouse looked like it always had—plain walls, dented roll-up door, no sign of the blood that had dried inside. Junior sat at a folding table with two of his boys, burner phones stacked beside unopened Topo Chicos. The TV played muted news. A silence lingered in the room, thick as tar.

Then—

A knock.

Not loud. Not frantic. Just deliberate.

Junior stood, peeked through the slat.

Benavidez.

He opened the roll-up halfway and stood in the shadow.

"You're a hard man to find," Benavidez said.

"Wasn't hiding," Junior replied. "Just busy."

"We need to talk," Márquez added, stepping beside her partner.

Junior didn't move. "About what?"

Benavidez crossed his arms.

"We know Manny's dead. We know your crew didn't just roll over and disappear. What we don't know is who you're working with—and how far this goes."

Junior tilted his head.

"You think I'm working with someone?"

Benavidez nodded. "Cartel fingerprints are all over this city. You may not be holding the knife, but you're cleaning up the blood."

Junior stepped out into the open. "I didn't start this."

"No," Benavidez said. "But you're still standing."

Junior's voice didn't rise. It didn't need to.

"I'm still standing because I've seen how this ends if you don't move smart. I'm not out here slinging dope on corners. I'm trying to keep people from burning down everything left."

Márquez narrowed her eyes. "By letting Los Cuervos run wild?"

Junior smirked, "What is that, a beer?"

She squinted at him, "Baboso."

Benavidez leaned in. "You think we haven't seen the bodies? The feathers in their mouths? You think we don't know who's cleaning house for Tico?"

Junior's grin faded. "I think you're talking to the wrong person."

He stared at them for a beat too long.

"We're done here."

Benavidez stepped forward once more. "You don't want to end up like Manny, kid. Buried under your own silence."

Junior shrugged.

"I'm not the one with a badge. You should worry about who isn't staying silent."

He started to pull the door down. Then stopped.

"Oh—and if the streets go quiet again, detective? Don't assume it's peace."

He let the roll-up slam shut.

"The wind that swings the dead whispers louder than any living tongue: fear is the new gospel."

—Book of the Forgotten, 19:7

Willow Street Bridge

Weeks had passed. The killings hadn't stopped—they had evolved.

In the story of David and Goliath, David wins, but not in this one. Here, Goliath wears silk shirts, a gold Rolex and Gucci sunglasses, and a gold plated 1911 .38 Super.

This wasn't corner warfare anymore. This wasn't about turf or who repped what color. The violence had changed—colder, more calculated.

People whispered about Juárez.

Bodies hanging from bridges.
Signs carved into skin.

Killings meant not just to silence, but to terrify.

Now, Bellavista was starting to feel the same.

Gunfire replaced crickets at night. Sirens played backup to the hum of transformers and late-night static. Law enforcement was drowning in calls, stretched thin, and some just looked the other way. And those who didn't—knew better than to knock twice on certain doors.

The line between gang and cartel had disappeared. What replaced it was something bigger. Crueler. A new kind of law, written in fear.

The call came just before sunrise.

Two bodies. Naked. Bound at the wrists and ankles. Headless. Hanging from the Willow Freeway overpass like meat left to rot in the wind. Swaying above stopped traffic. Anonymous, but not for long.

Benavidez stood at the edge of the tape, hands on hips, eyes locked on the bodies.

CHP had shut down both sides of the freeway. Drivers leaned against their hoods in stunned silence, kids held close. A few whispered prayers. Others just stared—trying to decide if this was real or some bad dream stuck between reruns of the nightly news.

Fire rescue worked slowly, almost reverently, lowering the bodies one at a time. The coroner's van waited nearby, doors yawning open like a hungry mouth.

Marquez stood just behind him, arms crossed, jaw tight.

As a Tech began placing one of the bodies into a bag, Benavidez stepped up to ID the bodies.

"Shit," he muttered.

Marquez came closer.

"Recognize them?"

He nodded slowly.

"Yeah. Prieto and Casper. Top dogs in Eastside Malditos." He recognized the visible tattoos that he had memorized from their sleeves.

Marquez stared at the blood-caked restraints, the bruises, and crude wounds carved into flesh.

"Jesus," she whispered, pulling out a bandana from her back pocket and placing it over her nose and mouth, trying to block the stench of iron and flesh.

"What now?"

Benavidez didn't blink.

He didn't answer right away. Just stood there, remembering how the wind had twisted their bodies like marionettes—stripped of control, moved by invisible hands.

"This ain't a message," he said flatly. "It's a blueprint."

Marquez turned toward him. "A blueprint for what?"

"For how they plan to run this city."

They watched in silence as the last of the bags was lifted into the coroner's van, its doors slamming shut like a judge's gavel.

"We're not ready for this," Marquez muttered.

Benavidez shook his head.

"We were never supposed to be."

She looked over. "So what now?"

He squinted toward the sunrise, the first orange light crawling over the cracked skyline.

"Now?" he said. "Now we dig in."

She glanced over. "Against who? We still can't even name them."

Benavidez cracked his neck, voice low and tired.

"We don't have to name them, Marquez. They already know who we are."

Across the road, beyond the yellow tape and uniformed officers, a solitary figure stood beneath a flickering lamppost.

Hoody pulled low, hands in his pockets. Silent. Watching.

Benavidez caught his eye.

Neither flinched.

Just a moment—long enough to acknowledge the invisible lines that had been drawn. One on the side of law, the other somewhere deeper in the shadows.

Marquez noticed. "Who's that?"

Benavidez didn't answer right away. He kept his eyes on him.

"Junior."

Then he turned back toward the van. The sun was just breaking now—splashing light over Bellavista like it didn't know any better.

Benavidez pulled on his sunglasses.

"Come on, let's go."
They walked off without another word.

Junior remained, unmoving, as the scene slowly cleared.

Two bodies. Two warnings.

But this wasn't the end.

This was just the silence before the city turned its face again—toward something colder, harder… inevitable.

And from that shadowed curbside, Junior understood what his place was now.

Not a soldier.

Not just another name in someone else's war.

He wasn't hiding anymore. He was watching. Measuring. Waiting.

This time, he would write the next chapter himself.

"The heads of kings are but coins in the bag; their silence buys obedience, their gaze buys fear."

—Book of Judgment, 15:3

The Duffle Bag

Officer Ruiz Memorial Park used to be a place for quinceañeras and church cookouts. Now it was just rust and graffiti—broken swings creaking in the wind and a busted water fountain that hadn't worked in years.

Word had gone out hours ago:

Sundown. Park. Come unarmed.

They showed. About twenty of them. The last of the Eastside Malditos. Leaderless. Twitchy. Waiting for someone to tell them how they were going to survive tomorrow.

Two black Suburbans rolled in slow. Headlights off. Tinted windows, engines humming like distant thunder. They parked. Doors opened.

Los Cuervos stepped out first—black silk shirts, twin gold-plated 1911s under their coats. Their faces unreadable. Their presence louder than gunshots.

Then came Junior.

Hood down. Chin up.

Not cocky. Just certain.

He walked ahead while the Cuervos fanned out behind him like shadows that had learned how to bleed.

One of the EM soldiers—young, scar across his neck—tried to square up.

"Where's Manny?" he asked, defiant.

Junior didn't flinch.

"Dead. Just like your leaders."

The words landed heavy. A few heads turned. Some lowered. Nobody stepped forward.

"I'm not here to negotiate," Junior continued. "I'm not here to explain anything. I'm here to give you a choice."

He gestured behind him. A Cuervo stepped forward and dropped a duffel bag on the cracked pavement between them.

Unzipped it halfway. Then stepped back.

The smell hit first—copper and rot. Then the faces.

Two heads. Eyes wide open. Muzzles of duct tape peeled back to show broken teeth and severed tongues.

Prieto. Casper.

No one spoke. No one moved.

"You think this is some kind of movie?" Junior asked, voice flat. "It's not. This is real. This is what happens when you think you can go toe-to-toe with La Sombra Negra."

He let the silence hang there like smoke.

"You got two options. Option one—walk away. Go home. Maybe even wake up tomorrow. Option two—you fall in line. You join LVG. You move our product. You follow our rules."

A pause. Then:

"What's in it for us?" one kid asked, barely old enough to shave.

Junior didn't blink.
"Protection. Money. Power. And a reason to still be breathing next week."

Another Cuervo stepped forward. Quietly zipped the duffel shut. Lifted it and tossed it into the back of a Suburban like it was trash.

More silence.

Then a pair of blue EM rags dropped to the ground.

Another followed. And another.

They didn't speak. Just walked forward. One by one. Head low. Pride swallowed. Fear heavy in their bones.

By the time the streetlights flickered on, the Eastside Malditos were gone.

And in their place, stood a new chapter of LVG.

Not louder.

Just deadlier.

And Junior?

He didn't say anything else.

He just turned. Walked back to the Suburban.

Los Cuervos followed.

And Bellavista bent quietly under a new kind of rule.

Longing for Home

A few months had passed.

The streets of Bellavista had returned to normal—at least, on the surface.

Men and women were back at work, navigating the usual stresses of life. Bills. Gas. Rent.

But in the back of their minds, the memories lingered.

Whispers of what had happened.

Shadows that didn't fade, just learned to blend.

On every block, the scars remained.

A tire shop—once an Eastside Malditos front—stood empty now.

Windows boarded.

Bullet holes tattooed across the stucco.

Chunks of concrete still missing from the sidewalk.

A few glints of glass caught the light, scattered like forgotten shrapnel.

All of it boxed behind chain-link and faded NO TRESPASSING signs.

Other buildings wore the same wounds.

Some tagged over.

Others left untouched—like shrines.

They were reminders.

Of how fast everything could collapse.

Of how quiet the city can be when the devil's already claimed it.

And through it all, the people watched.

Not because they didn't care.

But because there was nothing else they could do.

Bellavista no longer belonged to its families, its workers, its neighbors.

It belonged to La Sombra Negra.

And the cops?

They watched, too.

Powerless to stop the force that now owned the silence.

At Konig's, Rafa stood behind the counter, shoulders slightly hunched, eyes fixed on the computer screen. He was punching in part numbers—orders for parts the shop needed to finish jobs still waiting in the bays.

Chuy had stepped up as shop manager, the guy everyone went to now when something needed fixing—or someone needed direction. Rafa had finally been given the title of general manager. A consolation prize, maybe. Or a gesture of good faith. Either way, it was something.

Konig was gone.

Retired. Packed his bags and caught a flight north, trading Bellavista's smog and noise for Utah's cold skies, higher mountains, and cleaner air. Better hunting, too—at least that's what he'd said with a smile before disappearing.

The shop, with all its moving parts and history, was left in the hands of his nephew.

Rafa never talked about it, but it showed in the way he carried himself now. Slower. Quieter. The dream of one day owning the shop was gone—not with a bang, but with a signed retirement letter and a new name on the lease.

He didn't fight it.

He just kept working.

Because that's what Rafa did.

The front door chimed.

Rafa didn't look up. Eyes still on the screen, fingers tapping the keyboard.

"Can I help you?"

"Hola, papá."

That voice—soft, familiar, uncertain.

Rafa froze. His hands hovered above the keyboard.

"How are you?" Junior asked.

Rafa exhaled through his nose. A long pause.

"¿Ay, mijo… pues qué te puedo decir?"

He slid his glasses off and finally looked up.

The young man standing in front of him wore different skin now. Sharper lines. Heavier eyes. The streets had carved something new out of him. But somewhere in that face— buried behind the weight of time and choices—Rafa saw a flicker.

Just a flicker.

The boy he used to know.

And in his son's eyes—behind the cool posture and calm tone—was something else.

A silent, desperate plea.

The kind only a father could recognize.

A boy, lost in a storm, quietly asking to come home.

"How's Mom?" Junior asked. "I haven't seen you guys in a while."

Rafa nodded slowly. "Tu mamá está bien. She's been asking about you. She wants to know how you've been."

There was a long pause.

Rafa looked down, pretending to brush something off the counter—anything to hide the way his voice threatened to break.

"She misses you, mijo. She worries about you."

"I know, Pops." Junior's voice softened. "Tell her I'm okay… and that I miss her too."

Rafa nodded again, slower this time. The silence between them held weight—but not anger. Something closer to longing.

Junior cracked a faint smile.

"You think I could stop by for Sunday dinner? I miss her mole."

Rafa looked up—this time with something in his eyes. Not quite forgiveness. But something close.

"Claro que sí," he said, voice low. "Just don't be late. You know how she gets."

Junior's eyes lit up with excitement, "I'll bring a six pack of Modelo." Then turned and walked out the door.

Just before it closed, he looked back.

"I miss you, Pops."

The chime rang softly behind him.

Rafa didn't answer. He just stood there, glasses in hand, watching his only son walk away. His lips trembled. His eyes glossed. He clenched his jaw, willing the ache in his chest to behave.

Then—

The door between the lobby and the bays burst open.

"Rafa! Did the parts for the BMW get here yet?" Chuy asked, holding the door wide.

Rafa cleared his throat, voice a little too sharp. "When the parts get here, I'll let you know!"

Chuy blinked, caught off guard. He stood in the doorway for a beat.

Behind him, the low purr of a Mercedes rolled down the lot and faded into the street.

Chuy looked back at Rafa.

The old man was still staring out the window, jaw set, shoulders tight.

Chuy didn't say anything.

He just nodded once. "Okay, Don Rafa."

Then he slipped quietly back into the bays.

The Green Box

Later that evening, Junior drove through the heart of Bellavista.

The sun was beginning to dip behind the rooftops, casting long shadows over chain-link fences and faded murals. Streetlamps flickered to life, waking to watch over the night. Warm air clung to the pavement, and with it came the sounds of a city in motion—kids on bikes, skateboards rattling over sidewalk cracks, the occasional distant bark of a dog.

Parents watched from windows—close, quiet, alert. Ready to call their kids in at the first sign of trouble.

But tonight, like most nights lately, there wasn't any.

With only one crew now running the streets, there was peace—

or at least, a version of it.

The only real threats were junkies and lost souls wandering through alleyways. And LVG? They handled problems faster than BPD ever could. Quieter, too. Cleaner. If neighbors ever saw anything…

they didn't.

And life went on.

As Junior turned the corner onto Industrial, his eyes caught the faded white Grand Marquis parked near the loading dock.

His chest tightened.

For a second—just a second—his heart dropped into his stomach.

Old reflex.

Old ghosts.

But then he recognized the plate. The scent of new oil and cleaner. The faint hum of music through the roll-up.

Home base.

He pulled in, killed the engine, and stepped out.

Inside, the warehouse was lit in amber—low fluorescents humming above crates and tool benches. And at the center of it all, standing with his back to the door—

Tico.

"¡Junior!" he called, spinning around. "Hermano, ¿cómo estás, cabrón?"

His smile was real. His arms wide.

He walked up, threw one arm around Junior's shoulder and pulled him in tight. The hug of a boss, maybe. But more than that… of someone who meant it.

For that moment, whatever weight Junior carried—

it eased.

The doubt.
The worry.

Even the shadow of that old Grand Marquis.

Gone.

As they walked toward the conference room, the warehouse pulsed with quiet efficiency.

In one corner, young women sat at folding tables, counting thick stacks of cash, rubber bands snapping as bundles piled up. Across the way, a few LVG soldiers unpacked bricks of dope from duffle bags—carefully cutting, weighing, and sealing for the night's drops.

Business. As usual.

In the short time Junior had been running the operation, he'd tightened the screws on everything. His crews moved smart—small groups, clean hands, tight circles. Product was moved through stash houses scattered across Bellavista and beyond, each one anonymous, each one secure.

The streets ran quieter now, Junior's streets.

Flaco stood nearby, leaning against a steel post, arms crossed. Once one of Manny's most loyal soldiers, now Junior's right hand—loyal to a fault. If Junior gave the word, Flaco would burn half the city without blinking.

He nodded as they passed. Junior nodded back.

Respect. Earned, not handed.

As they stepped into the conference room, Tico motioned toward a chair.

"Siéntate, carnal—we got a lot to talk about."

Junior moved toward one of the side seats, but Tico gestured again, firmer this time.

"This is your house now, carnalito. You take that seat."

Junior hesitated. His eyes flicked to the head of the table—Manny's old spot.

Confused, he stood and slid into the chair.

Tico took the seat to his right and leaned back, a slow grin spreading across his face. His gold tooth flashed under the sterile flicker of the overhead lights.

He didn't speak right away.

Instead, he reached into the inside pocket of his charcoal western-cut blazer, the shoulders and chest paneled in jet-black ostrich leather—textured, rare, and unmistakably expensive. The jacket clung to him like authority stitched in fabric. Beneath it, a black silk shirt lay open at the collar, and around his neck hung a thick gold chain, weighted with a diamond-encrusted San Judas pendant that caught the light with every move. He laid a worn, cedar-lined cigar case on the table. From his other pocket came a gold-plated torch and a matching cutter—ornate, heavy, unmistakable.

The same set Junior had seen once before, back at the ranch.

Tico opened the case with care and plucked out a single Cohiba. He rolled it between his fingers with reverence, like it was a relic. Then he raised it to his nose and inhaled deeply.

Cedar. Spice. Leather. Cocoa.

The scent of ritual.

The scent of power.

That cigar had been hand-rolled by some old abuela in Cuba, her fingers stained from years of working leaves, her hands steady from a lifetime of precision.

Tico closed his eyes for a beat.

Like he wasn't just smelling the cigar—he was remembering everything that came with it.

Everything it meant.

Tico opened his eyes and looked at Junior.

A quiet chuckle slipped from his lips as he clipped the end of the cigar with the gold cutter.

"Mira," he said, almost like a sigh.

He brought the torch to the foot of the cigar and began to toast it, rotating slowly, precisely, letting the flame dance across the tobacco until the edges turned a dusty white. Then he placed it between his lips and took a deep draw.

The cherry flared bright red.

He held the smoke in his mouth, tasting it—rich, layered, slow.

Then exhaled.

The fragrance curled into the air—cedar and spice, a hint of cocoa. It wasn't harsh. It was warm. Familiar. The kind of smoke that lingered in the walls of back rooms and power moves.

"You've come a long way, carnal," Tico said finally, his voice low and steady.

"Ever since we lost Manny... you stepped up big time."

He paused to take another draw, then continued—

"I noticed it. And more importantly—

La Sombra Negra noticed it."

He blew the smoke upward this time—watching it swirl beneath the fluorescent light.

Tico looked around for somewhere to ash his cigar.

Junior caught it right away, stood up.

"Flaco—bring an ashtray from the other room for Tico. Ándale."

Flaco moved fast. Within seconds, he returned with a glass ashtray and placed it gently on the table.

Tico laughed, shaking his index finger at Junior.

"You see? That's what I'm talking about. Tú tienes buen control aquí."

Junior sat back down, fighting the urge to smile.

"So," Tico continued, brushing ash into the tray,

"because of that, el mero jefe has decided to send you more men. And double your output."

Junior blinked.

That landed heavier than he expected.

Tico stood, calmly placing the cigar case, cutter, and lighter back into the inside pocket of his ostrich-skin sport coat.

"And you know what that means?" he added, adjusting his sleeves.

"More money for you, hermano..."

His face shifted—warmth cooling into a more serious tone.

"...and more responsibility. But I know you can handle it."

Junior stood as well, falling in step beside him.

They walked past the roll-up doors, the warehouse humming behind them—men counting, packing, moving. Business.

As they approached the Grand Marquis, Tico lifted a hand. His driver opened the trunk and retrieved a small green box.

Tico turned and handed it to Junior.

A Rolex box.

Green leather. Embossed waves. The golden crown gleaming at the base.

Junior's eyes widened. He'd seen boxes like this behind glass. On billboards. Maybe once on someone's wrist at a wedding— but never up close. Never his.

He took it slowly, like he was holding a lit stick of dynamite.

Tico clapped him on the shoulder.

"Take it," he said. "You've earned it."

Junior nodded and opened the box.

Inside, nestled in cream velvet, sat the watch.

An 18k gold Rolex Day-Date "El Presidente"—black face, diamond incrusted dial. The kind of piece that didn't just tell time—it told everyone else who you were.

He lifted it, surprised by the weight. It wasn't just metal. It felt... permanent.

He stared at his own reflection in the sapphire crystal. For a second, he didn't recognize the man looking back.

"Manny would've liked it," Junior muttered.

"Manny never got one," Tico said flatly. "You did."

Junior looked at him—surprised.

But Tico just stepped into the back seat of the Marquis without another word.

The door shut.

The engine rumbled to life.

And just like that, he was gone—

Disappearing into the dark like the ghost of a king.

Junior stood there, clutching the box, feeling the bracelet cool in his palm.

It didn't feel like a gift.

It felt like a crown.

And now he had to wear it.

"Every table where bread is broken may also serve as an altar where destinies are weighed."

—Book of the Forgotten, 33:1

The Sit-down at Jaime's

"You hungry?" Benavidez asked, flipping his badge back into his coat.

Marquez looked up from her phone. "Mm, sure."

"Where you wanna go?"

She didn't hesitate. "Jaime's."

"Jaime's? Again?" he groaned. "We were just there."

"I don't give a shit," she said, buckling her seatbelt. "I want Jaime's Burgers."

Benavidez gave her a long, side-eye look, shook his head, and pulled out of the lot. "Alright, fine. Just don't ask me to lie when you're wondering why your pants don't fit."

She smirked. "Careful, viejo. Your knees don't work like they used to."

As they rolled up to Jaime's, the place was calm. Late afternoon crowd. A few regulars. The familiar scent of grilled onions and carne asada in the air.

Then Benavidez spotted him.

Corner booth.

Back against the wall.

Bottle of Topo Chico sweating on the table beside a half-eaten plate of fries.

Junior.

"Shit," Benavidez muttered.

"What?" Marquez asked, craning her neck.

"That's Junior."

"Oh," she said, lowering her sunglasses. "He's still pretty."

Benavidez shot her a look. "Keep it professional."

She smirked again. "Tell your blood pressure."

Benavidez approached the booth slowly, like a man sizing up a poker table before he sits.

"Mind if we join you?" he asked.

Junior didn't flinch. "You gonna eat or interrogate?"

Benavidez slid into the opposite side. "That depends. You gonna share your fries or your secrets?"

Junior tilted his head slightly. "One's salty. The other—dangerous."

Marquez pulled up a chair and sat with her arms crossed, scanning the place like backup on standby.

Benavidez leaned forward.

"You know, when I worked with your pops at Konig's, he used to say you had soft hands. Said you were meant for cleaner work—maybe college, a real trade. Something away from grease and steel."

Junior gave a dry chuckle. "Funny. He never said that to me."

"Probably didn't want to lie to your face."

Junior popped a fry into his mouth, chewed slow.

"You came here for the burgers or the guilt trip?"

"I came here," Benavidez said, "to remind you the walls are closing in. Slowly. Quietly. And one day, you'll hear a knock you can't ignore."

Junior leaned forward too now. Calm. Measured. Dead in the eyes.

"You had your chance with Manny. You watched the city bleed and stood there with your hands in your pockets. Now you wanna play fireman?"

"Manny was different," Benavidez said. "He knew where the lines were."

Junior's tone sharpened. "And look where that got him."

Silence fell. The kind that made the buzz of the fluorescent lights feel louder than it should've.

A kid laughed outside. A car alarm chirped. The line cook cursed in Spanish from behind the counter.

Benavidez tapped his fingers against the Formica table. "You're smart. Smarter than most that walk into this life."

"Is that supposed to be a compliment," Junior asked, "or a warning?"

"Both."

Benavidez leaned in closer.

"Smart ones die slower."

Junior stared, expression unreadable. Then he slid his tray aside and stood.

"I ain't Manny," he said. "I don't need to know where the lines are."

Benavidez nodded slowly.

"Just remember—when you cross 'em, you don't get to come back."

Junior turned to walk out. Paused halfway.

"Oh—and next time you want a sit-down," he added over his shoulder, "order your own damn fries."

The bell above the door jingled softly as he walked into the fading light.

Marquez leaned back in her chair, arms still crossed.

"You still think he's just a kid playing gangster?" she asked.

Benavidez didn't answer right away. Just watched the door slowly settle shut behind Junior.

"No," he said finally, reaching for a fry. "He's something else now."

"Great," Marquez said, "Can we order food now? I'm freaking starving."

"Pinche gorda."

"Callate baboso."

"The silence between father and son weighs heavier than any belt or bullet— for it buries love alive."

—Book of the Forgotten, 41:3

The Cost of Silence

Junior stepped onto the porch of his childhood home, a six-pack of Modelo in one hand, the other pushing open the creaky screen door that had never quite latched right. The familiar scent of cumin, fresh cilantro, and something slow-cooked greeted him like a warm embrace.

Inside, his amá turned from the kitchen, her face lighting up.

"¡Mijo!" she said, arms already reaching.

Junior leaned in, kissed her on the cheek. "Hola, amá."

She squeezed his arm lovingly. "Me da mucho gusto verte, mi amor."

He moved further into the living room, saw Rafa seated at the table, flipping through a local circular like he was going to buy something from it.

"I brought the Modelos," Junior said with a grin, raising the six-pack.

Rafa smiled wide, the kind of smile Junior hadn't seen in a long time. "¡Sí, sí! Pásate, mijo."

Junior set the beer down and looked around. The worn couch, the dent in the hallway drywall from when he launched a soccer ball too hard, the faint sound of Los Bukis playing low from the radio in the kitchen.

It hit him like a wave—childhood.

He could see flashes: G.I. Joes scattered across the rug, Saturday morning cartoons in his pajamas, the clang of the spoon against the bowl as his mom stirred pancake batter on Sunday mornings. The laughter. The security. The love—quiet, but ever-present.

The smell of mole broke his trance, rich and layered, pulling him toward the kitchen.

"Mom… it smells amazing!" he said, stepping in.

His mom stood at the stove, apron on, hair pinned back, stirring the thick, dark mole with her wooden spoon. She beamed when he walked in.

"¿Y las tortillas?" Junior teased.

"Hechas a mano," she said proudly, "like always."

The joy on her face filled the kitchen, and for a moment, the world outside didn't exist.

Junior walked back into the living room with two sweating Modelos in hand. He passed one to his dad.

"Toma, viejón," he said with a smile.

Rafa reached up and took it. "Gracias," he replied, settling deeper into his chair, eyes half on the TV.

They sat in comfortable silence, the kind that only fathers and sons can share after time and tension have slowly started to ease.

After a moment, Rafa chuckled softly, then looked over.

"¿Te acuerdas? When you were maybe five or six—playing with that soccer ball right here. Y tu mamá shouted, '¡Deja de jugar con esa pelota en la casa!'"

Junior grinned, already remembering.

"And I kicked it anyway and cracked the wall."

They both laughed—deep, full—the kind of laugh that came not just from the gut, but from a place of relief. A laugh that said, Yeah... we've been through some shit. But we're still here.

Junior took a swig of his beer and leaned back. The moment stretched, warm and simple.

"A ver, muchachos, ya está lista la comida," Junior's mom called from the kitchen. "¡Apúrense, or it's going to get cold!"

Rafa grunted as he got up, "Ya vamos," and they both shuffled into the kitchen like they used to on Sundays long ago.

Rafa took his place at the head of the small dining table, Junior to his right. The table was modest but full—love and labor plated in every dish. Mamá brought over a clay pot still steaming, the mole inside rich and dark with flecks of sesame floating at the top. Alongside it, she placed a basket of hand-pressed tortillas wrapped in a clean cloth, still warm and soft to the touch.

For a moment, no one moved.

Then—something rare.

"Rafa," Mamá said gently, "por favor, da la bendición."

Rafa blinked, surprised. It had been years since she'd asked him to give grace. Maybe even before Junior left home. But he nodded.

He reached across and grabbed his wife's hand, then looked at Junior. Junior paused, then extended his hand too, completing the circle.

Rafa bowed his head.

"Señor," he said quietly, "gracias por esta comida. Por mi esposa. Por mi hijo. Que sigamos teniendo estos momentos... porque no hay nada más importante que esto."

He squeezed both their hands gently, voice steady but low with emotion.

"Amen."

"Amen," they echoed.

And for a moment, everything was whole again.

The meal began like all good ones do—with silence, the kind born from reverence and hunger. Mole spooned over rice, chicken falling off the bone, tortillas passed hand to hand.

Laughter came easy after the first few bites.

"¿Te acuerdas cuando Junior se escondió en el clóset por tres horas porque rompió el florero de tu abuela?" Mamá asked, nearly choking on her horchata from laughing.

"I was six!" Junior protested, mouth half full. "Y ese florero ya estaba quebrado, nomás se cayó otra vez."

Rafa laughed, pointing his fork. "No, mijo, you tried blaming the dog—and we didn't even have one!"

They all burst out laughing again.

Later, Rafa poured a second round of Modelos and toasted with his son. "Salud, por los que estamos aquí… y por los que se nos adelantaron."

Junior clinked his bottle gently. "Salud, jefe."

The stories kept flowing. Junior talked about the time he snuck into the movies with a childhood friend and ended up watching the same film three times because they couldn't figure out how to leave without getting caught. Rafa told the story of how he first met Mamá—how she rejected him for a year straight until he showed up at her door with a guitar and a busted-up love song. She rolled her eyes and shook her head but couldn't help the smile that came with it.

The food slowly disappeared. Plates were cleaned with tortillas. The mole pot sat nearly empty. The kitchen grew quieter, softer, as if even the walls were listening.

Outside, the sun had long since disappeared. Crickets buzzed softly through the open window, a warm summer breeze rustling the curtains.

Rafa leaned back in his chair, hand on his stomach. "Dios mío… your mother's mole still hits like a freight train."

Junior nodded, a slow smile creeping onto his face. "Yeah," he said, glancing around the kitchen. "Feels like old times."

Mamá stood at the sink, her back to them, quietly washing dishes as if she didn't want to interrupt the moment, humming a tune that only she knew.

And for a few hours, everything was still.

Everything was right.

Until Junior's phone rang.

That ominous ringtone broke the warmth like a cold gust through an open window. The room, seconds ago filled with laughter and love, fell into a hush.

Rafa's smile faded. Mamá stopped washing dishes. Junior didn't move—just sat there, hand hovering over his pocket, eyes locked with his father's. For a beat, neither spoke.

Then Rafa looked away, trying to mask the weight in his chest.

Junior finally answered.

"Hello?... Simón, I'll meet you there."

He hung up and stood slowly. The chair scraped gently against the tile.

"Amá," Junior said, his voice soft. "Gracias por la cena. It was really good."

He walked over and placed both hands gently on her shoulders, kissed her on the cheek. She closed her eyes, held his hand a moment longer than usual.

Junior turned toward Rafa.

"Pops, I gotta head out. I got some—"

"Sí, sí," Rafa cut in, not looking at him. "Go take care of your business."

It landed like a slap across the table. Junior paused, unsure how to respond. So he didn't. He just nodded once and walked to the door.

Outside, the street was quiet. The air still held a bit of warmth from the day.

Junior slid into his Mercedes, turned the ignition, and sat there in silence.

Through the window, he watched his parents inside. Mamá and Rafa sat in the living room, the TV flickering across their faces. From a distance, it looked like peace—but only Junior knew the silence that had settled between them.

He rested his head back against the seat.

Then he turned the radio dial.

"Es un buen tipo mi viejo…"

"Que anda solo y esperando…"

The voice of Vicente Fernández poured into the cabin like a ghost—heavy with longing and guilt. Junior's eyes glistened as he stared at the house that raised him. A house full of memories. And now, tension.

He blinked away the moment. Turned the volume down. Shifted into drive.

And rolled into the night.

The night dragged on at the warehouse.

Packs were counted. Drops confirmed. Orders finalized. Junior moved through it all like a ghost in his own house— present, but distant. Flaco watched him with quiet concern but knew better than to ask.

The weight of leaving the dinner table still lingered in his chest. He could feel it behind his ribs, where the laughter used to be. A dull ache he couldn't shake.

By the time the first glow of dawn crept through the warehouse windows, the city outside began to stir. Birds in the rafters. Engines kicking over. Street dogs barking at garbage trucks.

Junior stood by the loading dock, staring out at the horizon, when his phone buzzed in his pocket.

He answered without checking the screen.

"¿Bueno?"

"Mijo…" his mother's voice cracked.

His stomach turned cold.

"¿Qué pasó, amá?"

There was a pause, then the weight of grief came through the line like a punch to the chest.

"Anoche tu papá y yo discutimos de ti… y en uno de esos—le dio un infarto."

Junior froze.

"No… no, no, ¿qué dijiste?"

Her sobs spilled through the speaker.

"Tu papá, mijo… ."

He felt the ground tilt. Everything around him faded.

"I'm on my way," he said, and the call ended before she could respond.

He turned and locked eyes with Flaco, "Flaco! It's my pops."

Flaco could see the concern in Junior's eyes, "I got you bro."

Junior ran to his car and sped off. He weaved in and out of traffic, running through every red light until he arrived at the hospital and stopped at the emergency entrance.

"Sir, you can't park there, it's for emergency vehicles only." A nurse had said.

He stared down the nurse who was wheeling a patient to an awaiting ambulance for transport, kept moving, ignoring the order.

Junior burst through the hospital doors, straight to the check-in desk.

"Hi—I'm looking for my dad. Uh, Rafael Quintero. He was brought in last night for a heart attack."

The receptionist began typing, her nails clacking softly on the keys.

"Yes. Mr. Quintero is in room 357, third floor." She slid a visitor pass across the counter. "Write your name and place it on your shirt. The nurse on three will point you in the right direction. Elevators are just down the hall to your left."

Junior quickly jotted his name on the badge and darted down the corridor, sneakers hitting tile with every urgent step, he slapped the badge on his shirt, spotted the elevators and mashed the up button.

"Come on, come on…"

When the doors finally slid open, a small crowd shuffled out. Junior weaved through them and hit the button for the third floor. The doors closed. Silence.

His thoughts swirled.

What do I say? Is he stable? What's he going to say to me?

What if…

The elevator dinged. The doors opened.

Ahead was the nurse's station.

"Room 357?" Junior asked, breathless.

The nurse nodded without looking up. "Straight down, past the restrooms. Take a right."

Junior nodded and moved fast. Heart pounding. Hands cold. He reached the room and stopped—just for a breath. Just long enough to pull himself together.

Then he turned the handle and stepped inside.

The beeping hit him first. That slow, steady rhythm that only meant one thing: life hanging on.

Rafa Quintero lay in the hospital bed. Tubes in his nose. IV in his arm. Monitors clipped to his chest. He looked pale. Older. Smaller somehow.

Junior's mom sat quietly at his side, hands folded in her lap. Her eyes found Junior's, wet with worry.

He stepped in, unsure of what to say—if anything at all.

"¿Qué quieres?" Rafa snapped, eyes still fixed on the window.

"Just want to know how you're doing, Pops," Junior said quietly as he stepped closer.

His mother sat silent beside the bed, eyes red, face drawn. She couldn't bring herself to speak.

Rafa turned slowly toward his son. His expression held no warmth.

"What does it matter, Junior?" he said, voice low but sharp. "Nada va a cambiar. What happened to me—last night—is just the consequence of your choices."

"Pops—"

"And don't tell me I don't know what I'm talking about," Rafa interrupted, tapping his temple with a trembling finger. "No soy pendejo."

The monitor beside him ticked upward—his heart rate climbing with every word. His face tightened in discomfort, his breathing shallow for a moment.

Junior stood frozen, unsure whether to speak or leave.

Rafa locked eyes with him. Behind the anger, behind the disappointment, was something even heavier: heartbreak. He loved his son with every fiber of his being—but he could not accept the life he'd chosen.

"Mijo… deja a tu papá descansar," his mother finally said, gently squeezing Rafa's hand.

Junior looked down at her—eyes filled with pain—then back toward his father.

Rafa had already turned away, staring again out the hospital window, as if the silence between them said more than words ever could.

"Okay, Mom," Junior said, his voice tight. "Me voy. Los amo mucho."

He turned and walked out, the hospital hallway feeling colder than before.

Whatever future lay ahead with his parents, he didn't know. But one thing was certain.

In the world he lived in—there was no turning back.

"The shepherd who tires of guarding wolves will one day bare his own fangs."

— Book of Judgment 14:9

The Fall of the Few

The night had come to a close. Benavidez and Marquez sat in silence as the cruiser rolled through the glowing streets of Bellavista. Sodium-vapor lights cast a warm yellow haze across cracked sidewalks, stretching shadows like ghosts. The engine hummed steadily beneath them, broken only by the occasional dispatch call crackling over the radio. Neither officer spoke. Their faces said enough—this was a city where power and money were king, and everything else had become an afterthought.

Benavidez pulled up to the gate behind the station and punched in the four-digit code. The keypad beeped. Behind them, the gate creaked open slowly.

Marquez picked up the mic. "David 15 to dispatch."

"Go ahead, David 15."

"Show us 10-19. We'll be 10-42 for the night."

"10-4, David 15. Welcome back."

The gate closed behind them with a finality that felt like a sigh. Benavidez pulled into a slot near the rear entrance, put the car in park, and just sat there. The silence settled heavy again.

"You okay?" Marquez asked.

Benavidez stared ahead, then turned and nodded faintly. "Yeah. I'm good."

She didn't believe it, but didn't press. "Cool. I'll see you in briefing." She stepped out, shut the door, and disappeared into the fluorescent wash of the station hallway.

Benavidez lingered. Then followed.

Inside, the station buzzed with life. Officers tapped away at keyboards, phones pressed to their ears, chasing down last-minute details on open reports. Jailers processed fresh bookings, the low moans of drunk tank detainees echoing off tile. Radios crackled in every corner. The machine of law enforcement never really stopped—it just sputtered into the early morning hours.

Benavidez walked into the briefing room. Sergeant Walker stood at the front, sleeves rolled, clipboard in hand.

"Alright, listen up," Walker barked. "Tonight was a win. Our stolen vehicle task force recovered two units—one matched to a home invasion from last month, other was clean. Good work on the impound, Alvarez."

The room gave a tired nod of acknowledgment.

But for Benavidez, it was background noise. Static.

His mind drifted—images and voices from the past few months looping like a scratched DVD. Güero bleeding out in front of Jaime's. Tico smiling like the devil in court-pressed slacks. Junior standing outside a church like he belonged there.

He sat quietly, trying to care.

But something inside had shifted. The line between order and chaos had blurred. And he couldn't tell if he was still one of the good guys—or just another cog in a broken machine.

When the briefing wrapped, Benavidez made his way to the locker room.

A few officers were gearing up for the next shift, others breaking down from theirs—unzipping vests, stowing radios, rubbing tired eyes as they prepared to head home. It was a quiet ballet, practiced and unconscious.

Benavidez opened his locker and began his ritual. He unstrapped his vest, heavy with hours and expectations, and hung it on the reinforced hanger inside. He reached for his Glock 17, cleared it, and holstered it into his appendix rig before setting it on the shelf. His duty belt followed—draped beside the vest like armor retired for the night.

Then he unclipped his shield from the belt.

He sat down on the bench and stared at it—just the shield, nothing else in that moment.

A slideshow played in his mind.

His first day at the academy—buzzcut, bright-eyed, not yet jaded.

His rookie year, forgetting everything he learned in the classroom and learning the truth on the streets.

The day he pinned on his detective badge—shocked he'd even passed the exam.

Then came the promotion—Detective Sergeant. A leader. A mentor.

Back when the unit was filled with passionate, sharp-eyed detectives who believed they could make a difference.

It was a different city back then.

The rules were simple: You're the bad guy. I'm the good guy.

You do something wrong, and I come find you.

But now?

Now the lines were smeared.

And if you crossed one, how would you even know?

And worse—did anyone care anymore?

His phone rang, snapping him out of the memory loop.

"Hello? …Yeah, I'll be home soon. Okay, sure. Love you too."

He stood, slid the shield into his locker, and quietly walked out.

The drive home was quiet, the kind of quiet that made your thoughts louder.

Benavidez gripped the steering wheel with one hand, the other resting loosely on the door, eyes scanning the same streets he'd driven for over two decades. The same cracked sidewalks. The same dim streetlights.

He thought about all the titles, the commendations, the cases he'd closed. All the arrests, the long hours, the paperwork, the moments where he thought—this matters.

"But what were they worth now?" he muttered to himself, voice barely above the hum of the engine.

What's the point?

Every time he tried to make a difference, the city just shifted around it. Like trying to carve your name into water.

And people like Junior?

They thrived in the chaos. Protected by the same community that turned its back on the badge. Revered. Untouchable.

He can do what we can't, Benavidez thought. *He's judge and executioner, saint and sinner. They love him for it. All I get is paperwork.*

He came to a stop at the red light on Soto and Lewis.

This corner was always alive after dark—the so-called "Night Life" of Bellavista. Bars spilling light onto cracked pavement. Music thumping behind tinted glass. Trouble hiding behind every neon sign.

To his left was Mariscos El Chepe—a local favorite for late-night seafood and drinks. Always packed. Always brimming with drama.

Benavidez glanced toward the front window—and froze.

There, in the center booth, lounged a familiar silhouette. Junior.

He sat like a king—arms stretched over the backrest, body language loose and untouchable. Around him, Flaco, along with a few LVG soldiers laughed and drank. Two women leaned close, draped in designer dresses and fake smiles. On the table: crystal-clear bottles of high-end tequila and deep amber brandy, catching the light like jewelry.

It was a scene ripped out of a narco-fantasy—wealth, women, protection.

And outside, in a twenty-year-old car, sat Benavidez. Hands tired from years of paperwork. Heart tired from a war no one wanted to win. Trying to keep his family afloat on a cop's salary. Surviving.

While men like Junior thrived—built empires on drugs, bullets, and blood.

His jaw clenched. His grip tightened around the steering wheel until the leather creaked.

"Motherfucker," he muttered under his breath.

The light turned green. He didn't move.

He kept his eyes on the glass window of El Chepe. Watched Junior raise a glass, toast his crew, laugh like he owned the night.

Benavidez swallowed hard. His throat felt dry. Maybe it was the heat from the vents, or the bile rising in his gut.

Twenty years I gave this city.

The academy. The partners he'd lost. The cases he bled for. The nights he didn't come home. The marriage that barely held together because he always put the job first.

And for what?

Junior lived untouched. A saint in the eyes of the community. Fed the poor, threw parties for the neighborhood, paid for funerals. Played the role of savior. Meanwhile, he moved dope like oxygen and buried bodies like receipts.

We build the case, the DA drops it.

We catch them dirty, Internal says it's not clean enough.

We try to stop it, the community shields him.

We try to warn them, they call us liars.

Benavidez gripped the wheel tighter.

What's the point of following the rules… if the rules are made to protect people like him?

For the first time in his career, the thought entered his mind with clarity—not rage, not impulse, but sober clarity:

Maybe it's time someone plays by his rules.

The radio squawked:

"Unit 12, respond to 415 at Boyle and Maple. Male subject throwing bottles into traffic."

Benavidez blinked. His hand moved, almost on instinct, toward the mic.

He hesitated. A breath. Then he let it go.

Another unit keyed up. "12's in route. Show us code three."

Benavidez shifted his cruiser into drive. Not toward the call. Not toward the station.

He turned down a side street instead—no lights, no destination. Just quiet.

The engine hummed beneath him like it always had. But it felt different now. Colder. Detached. Like the car no longer belonged to a cop, but to someone else entirely.

He drove without thinking, letting the city pass him by—storefronts, street corners, all the places he used to know. All the places he used to believe in.

Maybe it wasn't about breaking the rules.

Maybe it was about correcting the ones that never worked.

He thought about Junior again. Thought about the armor he wore—not bulletproof vests, but loyalty, fear, and image. No badge could penetrate that.

But a man could.

If he was willing to cross the line.

And Benavidez, for the first time in twenty years, didn't feel the weight of his oath.

He felt the weight of purpose.

Benavidez pulled into his driveway. The porch light cast a soft glow over the walkway, and through the blinds, he could see the living room light still on.

He sat there for a moment, staring at the front door.

Then he took a breath. Deep. Steadying.

Inside, his wife was on the couch, curled under a blanket with a book in her hands. She looked up as he walked in.

"Hi, babe. Sorry I'm late," he said, his voice low but even.

She smiled gently and nodded. No questions. Just presence.

He set his keys on the table and stood there for a beat too long, something stirring inside him—something he couldn't name yet. It felt foreign, like a warning… or maybe a spark.

Maybe it was time for a change.

Silhouettes at the Table

The sun hadn't fully crested the rooftops when Benavidez pulled up to the warehouse. The block was quiet—too quiet. No music. No movement. Just the soft hum of power lines overhead and the sound of his engine cooling after he killed the ignition.

He stepped out slowly, hand resting near his belt—not on his weapon, just near enough. He wasn't in uniform. Didn't wear the badge today. Just jeans, boots, and a flannel shirt—old school cop clothes. The kind worn by men who still believed in warnings before war.

He approached the roll-up door. Before he could knock, it rattled halfway open and Flaco appeared from the shadow like a watchdog on command.

"What do you want, homes?" Flaco asked, calm, but with that look in his eye that said the calm didn't last long.

"I'm looking for Junior," Benavidez said, voice low and direct.

"He's not here. Why don't you go look somewhere else?" Flaco's tone turned sharp—dismissive.

Just then, footsteps echoed from deeper inside.

Junior emerged from the hallway behind the office, hands still drying on a shop towel, like he'd just finished inventory. He saw the stance, the tension. He read it instantly.

"Flaco, calma," Junior said, nodding once. "Let him through."

Flaco didn't move at first. Then, after a long second, he stepped aside.

Benavidez walked past, shoulder brushing against Flaco on purpose, eyes never leaving him.

Junior opened the side door to the office. "We need to talk," Benavidez said. "In private."

"Sure thing. Come on in."

Before stepping inside, Junior turned to Flaco and added, "Don't let anyone interrupt us."

The door clicked shut behind them.

It was quiet inside. Dim. The blinds were drawn. One table. Two chairs. No desk. No glass of water offered. This wasn't hospitality — it was business.

Junior leaned against the wall. Benavidez didn't sit.

Benavidez: "You know why I'm here."

Junior: "Yeah. I do. But I'm curious which version of you showed up today. The one that still wears a badge... or the one that's tired of watching good people die for nothing."

Benavidez stepped closer, his jaw tight.

Benavidez: "Don't play that card with me. You think I don't know what this place is? What you've become?"

Junior: "What I've become?"

He let out a breath, almost a laugh.

"Nah, Benavidez. This city made me. You just weren't paying attention."

Benavidez didn't blink.

"I saw you last night. At El Chepe. Holding court like some kind of king. You had killers on one side and broken girls on the other. And you? Smiling. Like you're not the cancer."

Junior: "You still think I'm the problem?"

He stepped forward now. Not threatening — just real.

"Look around. The streets respect me more than they respect you. Why? Because I don't hide behind procedure. I get shit done. I keep the peace."

Benavidez scoffed. "By selling poison?"

"By controlling it." Junior fired back. "You want chaos or control? 'Cuz trust me, if I go down—this city burns."

Silence.

Benavidez's eyes studied him—long, hard, searching for something still human.

"There was a time I thought I could stop this. Thought the badge meant something."

Junior: "Maybe it did... before they gave promotions to paper-pushers and let the real ones bleed out in alleys."

Another beat.

Benavidez: "I'm not here to moralize. I'm here to make you an offer."

That got Junior's attention.

"Go on."

"I look the other way. Not because I want to... but because I know I'm losing. You keep your chaos contained. Keep it off the streets, away from schools, parks, families... and I let things slide."

Junior didn't smile. But something behind his eyes flickered — respect.

"That's a hell of a first step."

"It's not a partnership," Benavidez snapped. "It's survival. You give me peace in exchange for silence. One wrong move? I take you down myself."

Junior nodded slowly. Then said:

"Then welcome to the table."

Benavidez didn't shake his hand.

He turned and walked out, past Flaco, past the warehouse door, and into the morning light.

And behind him, Junior stood in the doorway, watching.

Two silhouettes.

Each having crossed a line they swore they'd never cross.

Benavidez stepped out into the sunlight without another word.

Junior stayed behind, the door closing softly behind him.

Flaco was leaning against the wall just outside the office, arms crossed, eyes sharp.

He watched Benavidez walk away in silence.

Then looked at Junior.

"What was that all about?"

Junior didn't answer right away. He let the question hang in the air as he stepped forward, stopping beside Flaco.

"That," he said quietly, "was an ace up our sleeve."

He patted Flaco on the shoulder.

A slow smirk crept across Flaco's face as he pushed off the wall.

"Orale."

The roll-up door buzzed shut behind them.

And inside, the game kept moving.

"Beware the sun when it smiles upon you, for its warmth is a warning dressed as a gift."

— Book of the Forgotten, 8:9

Crossing Shadows

It started like any other day in Bellavista.

The sun was at its highest, blazing down, heatwaves dancing above the cracked streets.

Junior sat in his office at the warehouse, watching the floor through the glass. LVG guys unpacked bricks, breaking them down for sale, the smell of gasoline and cellophane hanging in the air. On the far side, the women counted and stacked cash, wrapping it tight, ready for the run south to Tijuana.

The phone rang.

"Hello?"

"¿Qué honda, plebe? This is Tico."

"What's up, Tico? How's things in Tijuas?"

"Todo bien, carnalito. You know how it is—sometimes you gotta make a few heads roll to keep shit in line."

Junior knew the methods down south. Always had. He still prided himself on never needing that level of blood to keep order on his side of the border.

"Mira," Tico's voice dropped a notch, "I need you down at the ranch today. There's some things we need to talk about—in person."

"Simón, Tico. I'm headed out now."

Outside, the heat hit like a shove to the chest. Flaco was already by the truck, engine idling, sunglasses hiding his eyes.

"Where we going?" he asked without looking over.

"Tijuas."

Flaco smirked, slid the shifter into drive. "Orale."

The road south felt different this time.

Last time, riding shotgun with Manny, Junior had sat tight, reading every shadow as a possible threat, every glance from another driver like a challenge.

Not today.

Today, he sat back. One arm draped over the window frame, eyes on the horizon. A trip now part of the routine. The hum of the tires and the low growl of the motor were steady, confident. This wasn't a trip into the unknown—it was a trip deeper into territory he was starting to think of as his own.

The cityscape gave way to suburbs, then open highway. Palm trees bent under the wind. Semi-trucks rolled past heavy with cargo, some of it legitimate, most of it not.

They passed the spot where, months ago, he'd seen Disneyland's fireworks bleeding into the night sky—a reminder of how close fantasy and reality could live. Now? He didn't even glance.

By the time they hit Otay Mesa, Flaco had the process down like clockwork. He pulled into the first lane at the border, rolled the window down just enough for the guard to look in.

The soldier glanced at Flaco, then at Junior. Recognition flickered.

"Buen viaje, muchachos," the guard said with a short nod.

Flaco returned it and rolled forward.

Tijuana hit them in waves—the noise, the heat, the constant motion. His first time, Junior's eyes darted everywhere—tracking threats, taking in every story written on every street corner.

Now, he looked through it all, scanning like a man who knew where the lines were drawn and who drew them. He saw the hustlers, the drunks, the neon-lit girls leaning on doorways—not as danger, but as part of the machinery.

Thirty minutes later, they turned onto the cracked street that hid Tico's fortress.

The same ten-foot concrete walls. The same iron spikes. The same silent sentries with their Norinco rifles. Only now, Junior nodded to them first—and they nodded back.

When the gates groaned open, the willow-lined drive unfolded ahead. Junior remembered the first time, the way the place had felt like stepping into another world. It still did—but now, the weight of it settled on his shoulders differently. Less like intimidation. More like responsibility.

As the mansion came into view, Flaco cut the engine and glanced at him.

"Listo?"

Junior smiled faintly. "Always."

They stepped into the shade of the garden, the fountain's spray cooling the air. The carved mermaid's stone eyes seemed to follow him, but Junior didn't slow his pace.

Inside, the air was chilled, carrying the faint scent of citrus and polished wood. The marble under his boots gave off a muted echo with each step.

"Buenas tardes, señor Quintana," a maid said, passing by with a silver tray stacked with fresh towels. She didn't stop, didn't bow—just spoke with the respect of someone who knew who he was.

Junior nodded back. "Buenas."

They moved deeper into the house, past the open living room and its vaulted ceilings. One of the armed guards near the back doors straightened when he saw them, then offered a short, clipped "Señor."

Junior returned it with a look and kept walking.

The double doors to the patio were already open, letting in a warm breeze and the sound of water from the pool. Somewhere out near the stables, a stallion let out a sharp, commanding whinny.

They passed another staff member—this one a young man in an embroidered shirt, polishing a set of crystal decanters on a side table. He didn't look up, but his "A sus órdenes, señor" landed with the same quiet acknowledgment as the others.

By the time they reached the long wooden patio table, Junior could see Tico at the far end, leaning back in his chair like a man who owned every inch of ground they stood on.

Next to him sat Sebastian, the ever-composed finance man, posture perfect, a ledger open in front of him. A half-empty espresso cup rested at his elbow, the small silver spoon perfectly aligned on the saucer.

Tico raised his glass in greeting.

"Plebe… bienvenido."

Sebastian offered only a thin smile, tapping his pen once against the page before closing the ledger and sliding it aside.

Junior took the seat offered, Flaco standing just behind him. For the first time, the house, the land, and the people moving within it didn't feel like Tico's alone.

They felt… shared.

Tico studied Junior for a long moment, taking in the change—the way he carried himself now, the clothes, the cologne. It was like looking at a man who'd once shown up as nothing more than a larva, wrapped tight in his own cocoon, and now stood before him as a rising star in the underbelly of society.

He smiled.

"Look at you, carnalito… all grown up. Right, Sebastian?"

Sebastian gave a polite, knowing smile.

"I've come a long way, Tico. Been through some shit. But now—" Junior spread his arms, gesturing to the table, the house, the moment. "Here we are."

"Yes… indeed." Tico leaned back, a faint grin pulling at the corner of his mouth. "Here we are."

Sebastian opened the leather-bound ledger, flipping to a marked page.

"Last month you brought in $1.2 million. The month before—$1 million flat. Before that? Just over seven-fifty. I'd say you've been on a pretty good trajectory."

"You hear that, carnalito? 'A pretty good trajectory.'" Tico's gold tooth flashed as he grinned. "Sounds like you're doing well."

"Me alegra, carnal." Tico clapped his hands once, sharp and loud, before reaching for a bottle of Don Julio Blanco. He poured three heavy glasses.

All three men raised their drinks.

"¡Salud!" Tico roared, and they downed the shots in one motion.

Tico laughed, the sound rolling from deep in his chest. "¡Eso! Great job, carnalito. You've really impressed La Sombra Negra."

Junior was caught off guard by the compliment, but his face didn't show it. He kept his cards close.

"Is that so?" was all he said.

Junior set the empty shot glass down, the warmth of the tequila still lingering in his chest.

Tico leaned back in his chair, eyes fixed on him. "You ever hear the story of Icarus, carnalito?"

Junior shook his head.

"Not the one from the books — my way," Tico said, rolling the glass between his fingers. "There was this boy who wanted to touch the sun. His father warned him — fly too low and the sea will take you, fly too high and the sun will burn you. But the boy…" Tico smirked, "the boy wanted more. So he flew higher. And higher." He lifted his hand, palm flat, gliding it upward through the air as if riding an invisible current., "Thought he was untouchable."

Tico placed the glass on the table with a soft clink.

"Then his wings melted, and he fell. Straight into the sea." Without warning, he dropped his hand and smacked the table "Gone!" Tico snapped his fingers, "Just like that."

He leaned forward, voice low, steady.

"In this life, the sun is power. It'll make you feel untouchable. But if you start believing your own legend…" He tapped the table twice with his gold ring. "The fall is faster than the rise."

"That's why I'm telling you this now — because you, carnalito, are about to fly higher than you ever have."

Tico's smile returned, sharp and certain. "From today, you run everything — Tijuana, and California. Operations, collections, distribution. You answer only to me."

Junior didn't move right away. He let the weight of the words sink in.

Across the table, Sebastian closed the ledger with deliberate care, almost like sealing a deal. He gave Junior a slow nod — the kind that said this is big without a single word.

Even Flaco, still posted behind Junior's chair, shifted his stance ever so slightly, his eyes flicking between the two men at the table.

Tico leaned forward, resting his forearms on the table.

"I'll be moving up, al lado del mero jefe. Sebastian will stay here, help you manage the cash flow. Pero entiende esto…" He tapped the table twice for emphasis.

"He'll be working with you… but he works for me."

The words were calm, but iron sat under every syllable.

"That way, you have nothing to worry about — because his loyalty is with me, and he has my best interest at heart. And well…" a slow grin crept across his face, the gold tooth catching the light,

"carnalito, you are my best interest."

Sebastian gave a small, knowing smile — the kind that could mean reassurance… or a reminder.

Junior held Tico's stare, feeling the weight behind the words — the trust, the warning, the leash.

Finally, he nodded once. "Then we're on the same page."

The handshake that followed wasn't just agreement. It was a contract — unspoken, binding, and dangerous.

Tico leaned back, satisfied. "Así me gusta."

He raised his voice. "¡Rosa! Bring us food and a bucket of cold Modelos!"

Junior glanced back at Flaco and motioned for him to join them. Tico nodded his approval.

"A celebrar, muchachos."

The Weight of the Crown

"Hello?"

"Benavidez, it's Junior."

Benavidez rolled over, the phone cold against his ear. The red digits on the clock glared back at him: 3:04 a.m. The room was still, save for the low hum of the AC and the steady breathing of his wife beside him.

"It's three in the morning," he muttered. "What do you want?"

Junior's voice was calm, direct — like this was business hours. "Listen up — seven a.m., a white Corolla's coming in from Otay. All you gotta do is make sure it makes it safe and clear to the warehouse."

Benavidez rubbed his face, heartbeat loud in his own ears. He stared at the ceiling, the shadow of their last meeting heavy in his mind — the handshake, the unspoken terms, the promise that had shifted the ground under his feet.

"Fuck…" he breathed, the word hanging there for a beat.

Finally, he exhaled, the choice already made. "Okay. No problem."

The line went dead. Benavidez set the phone on the nightstand, staring at it like it had just taken something from him. He glanced over — his wife was sound asleep, her face peaceful, oblivious to what he had just stepped into.

Across the city, Junior would be sleeping soundly, knowing the message had landed.

By 7 a.m., Benavidez sat in his cruiser across the street, watching the white Corolla glide into the warehouse lot. The roll-up doors rattled open, swallowing the car whole like a shark taking its prey.

A moment later, the side door creaked open. Junior stepped out.

They locked eyes across the distance for a beat, no words —
Benavidez then turned, slid into his unit, and pulled away.

Half a block down, something caught his eye. On the
passenger seat sat a small manila envelope, like it had been
waiting for him.

"What the fuck!" he barked, slamming a palm into the steering
wheel, hard enough to sting.

Back at the warehouse, Junior stood in the sunlight, Ray-Ban
aviators shielding his eyes, hands on his hips. The smile across
his face said everything — the kind of smile you give when the
game is going exactly the way you planned.

Flaco appeared from across the street and walked over to
Junior, "It's done."

Junior nodded, still watching the street where Benavidez had
disappeared.

"Good. He's in now."

Flaco's grin widened. "For good?"

Junior finally turned toward him, the sunlight catching the edge
of his shades.

"For good."

He walked back inside, the cool shadows of the warehouse swallowing him as quickly as the roll-up doors had taken the Corolla. The floor was already alive with movement — LVG soldiers unloading packages, women at the counting tables stacking bills with the practiced precision of casino dealers.

The operation didn't pause for anyone — not even for a cop.

"Flaco, make sure that package is processed. I'll be in the office."

"Simón, patrón," Flaco said with a quick nod before heading toward the Corolla.

Junior unclipped his Nextel and chirped Sebastian,

"¿Bueno?"

"It's Junior. The package arrived without issues."

"Good. I'll let Tico know."

The line went dead. Sebastian never wasted words.

Junior clipped the Nextel back on his belt and stepped out onto the catwalk overlooking the warehouse floor. Below him, the operation moved like a living organism — soldiers unloading, women counting, cash stacking into neat bricks, the hum of a business that never slept.

He leaned on the railing, letting the weight of the moment settle in.

Everything he saw… he'd built.

Junior descended from the catwalk, weaving through the bustle. Flaco intercepted him mid-stride, handing over a clipboard.

"Shipment's clean, patrón. Everything's where it needs to be."

Junior nodded, scanning the sheet.

Then, his pocket buzzed. He pulled out his other phone — a chunky Nokia 5110, dark blue faceplate scuffed from years of use. The small green screen flashed Maribel.

"Hold on, I gotta take this," he told Flaco, handing the clipboard back.

He thumbed the answer button. "¿Qué onda, prima?"

"Junior, hey… do you have a minute?" Her voice was bright but a little nervous.

"Give me a sec to step outside — it's too noisy in here."

He pushed open the side door, the heat of the morning hitting him as the warehouse hum faded behind. Out on the loading dock, he leaned against the railing, watching the street while he listened.

"I wanted to ask you something," she said. "It's… kind of important."

Junior smiled. "What's up?."

"I was wondering if… you'd be the padrino for my quinceañera. I mean… of my shoes. I wish I could have a big celebration, but you know… my parents don't have much and—"

"Don't worry, little prima," he cut in, voice warm and certain. "No te faltará nada, I got you."

There was a pause, then a soft laugh from her end. "I knew you'd say yes."

"Of course I'd say yes. You're family."

They talked a few minutes more, Maribel bubbling with ideas — colors, songs, the dress she dreamed of, her favorite banda. Junior listened, picturing the little girl he'd seen grow up now stepping into her own moment.

When they finally hung up, he slipped the Nokia back into his pocket and stayed on the dock a beat longer. The street was quiet, but inside, the warehouse still roared — voices calling out counts, forklifts beeping, the clatter of money machines.

Two worlds. One he could walk into at any time, a place of power, respect, and danger. The other — family — he had to protect from the first at all costs.

He exhaled slowly, then stepped back inside. The noise swallowed him whole.

The danger of living a life of duality is that sometimes, you don't see the predators watching from behind the tall grass. They move slowly, patiently, hidden in the noise—waiting for the moment you let your guard down.

"Gold and glass can crown a man a king, but one careless spark can burn the throne."

— Book of Judgment, 21:6

Smoke & Mirrors

Flaco was waiting for Junior outside in the suburban. "Where we headed?"

Junior adjusted the sleeves of his guayabera, gold glinting from his watch. "Mercedes dealer. Time for an upgrade."

"Orale campeón, let's go."

They rolled past liquor stores, barbershops, old taco joints clinging to a different time. Junior watched the city blur by, his city now — and he was done playing checkers on someone else's board.

The Suburban rolled to a smooth stop in front of the glass-walled Mercedes-Benz dealership on Figueroa. All blacked out — windows, rims, paint — the kind of truck that didn't belong in a place like this. The kind that drew stares. Not admiration. Suspicion.

Flaco cut the engine. They stepped out like shadows — two young Mexican men, late twenties, walking with that mix of silence and swagger that made suits nervous. Inside the showroom, sunlight hit polished steel. Cars gleamed like trophies waiting for names.

A salesman spotted them through the glass, already sizing them up. Baggy jeans. Gold chains. Tattoos peeking under shirt sleeves. Goddamn cholos, he thought. Here to waste my time.

Junior stepped into the showroom and walked toward a silver sedan. He ran his fingers along the crisp body lines like he was testing the tension on a fine blade.

"That's the S500," the salesman offered as he approached, trying to stand between them and the nicer stock. "Top of the line. Epitome of luxury. Also, one of the most expensive models on the lot."

Junior gave him a cool glance, unimpressed by the pitch or the posture.

"That's a beautiful machine," he said evenly, his voice calm but unreadable.

Then he noticed the S600 tucked toward the back of the showroom, as if reserved for a different kind of buyer.

"Ey, Flaco," Junior called out. "Check that one out."

Flaco wandered over, eyeing the deeper grille and longer wheelbase. "Damn, this one's clean."

Junior turned to the salesman. "How much?"

The salesman crossed his arms, lips pinched. "One hundred and forty-five thousand dollars."

Junior smirked. Flaco raised his shoulders. Junior kept moving, cool as ever, eyes scanning the floor like he was still shopping.

Flaco grabbed a tri-fold brochure off the podium near the espresso machine. He flipped toward the back. "Hey, what's this? The S70 AMG?"

The salesman glanced at the page, then toward the S600. "That," he said with a sniff, "is an AMG. Specially tuned V12. Six hundred horsepower. It's a special-order vehicle. We don't stock those."

Junior turned, now fully interested. "How much?"

"Two hundred thousand," the salesman replied flatly, as if the number might shoo them off.

Junior looked at Flaco. Flaco looked back. No nods. No words. Just the quiet language of men who knew what they wanted.

"Do you take cash?" Junior asked.

That stopped everything.

The sales manager, half-listening from his desk, suddenly looked up. The salesman blinked, unsure if he'd heard correctly. Flaco was already heading back to the Suburban.

The sales manager stood. "Right this way, Mr...?"

"Quintana," Junior said, following him into the office.

Inside, the air felt different — calmer, quieter, but charged. The manager poured him a glass of water. Junior didn't touch it. He leaned back, arms draped casually, king-like.

Papers were drawn. Custom order confirmed.

Ten minutes later, the door opened. Flaco stepped in, briefcase in hand. He set it gently on the table and clicked it open. Neatly stacked bands of cash. No nonsense.

The manager's throat clicked as he swallowed. "We'll expedite the order. You'll be the first in Southern California to take delivery."

Junior stood and extended his hand. "Good. I like being first. Oh, and uh," Junior said with a smile, "make sure it's black on black."

They left the same way they came — quiet, deliberate, and watched.

Back in the Suburban, Flaco pulled into traffic. The city moved around them like background noise, unaware a new king had just signed his coronation papers.

"That was smooth," Flaco said, eyes on the road. "You see that salesman's face?"

Junior smirked, flipping through the S-Class brochure one last time before tossing it to the floor. "People like that never expect it."

Then — chirp.

"Ey boss, you better get here quick. Lil Smokey fucked up."

Junior looked over. Flaco was already changing lanes.

"On our way," Junior replied, his voice calm but clipped. Whatever high he was riding had just been dragged back to earth.

The Suburban cut through traffic like a blade. No music. No chatter. Just the hum of the engine and Junior's silence.

He stared out the window, jaw tight. It had to be Smokey. Always the ones you do favors for who can't keep their shit together.

They pulled up to the warehouse. A few of the guys were outside, pacing, smoking, not meeting Junior's eyes as they pulled up.

The look on their faces told a story nobody wanted to hear.

But Junior was about to find out inside.

The Crown That Cuts

Flaco brought the Suburban to a sharp stop outside the warehouse, tires chirping just enough to draw eyes. He was out before the dust settled.

"¿Qué hacen afuera? Get back inside—now!"

The group of soldiers scattered, moving quick. Junior stepped out just after, eyes scanning the yard. His pace was calm, but the weight behind it made people move.

Inside the warehouse, the heat clung thick. A silver Nissan sat parked awkwardly near the loading zone, its trunk popped open like a mouth mid-scream. Inside, limp and folded, was the body of a low-level dealer. Junior recognized him instantly—one of the runners from Wilmington. Sloppy but loyal. Or so he thought.

To the right, leaning against a steel support beam, stood Lil Smokey. His hands were crusted with dried blood. Tears streaked through the grime on his cheeks. Sweat dripped off his brow. Beside him, crumpled on the concrete floor, was a girl Junior had never seen before. Young. Shaking. Makeup smeared into ruin.

Junior's jaw tensed.

"Who's this?" he asked, voice level.

Smokey swallowed. "That's my girl. I had her with me at a stop."

Junior turned toward the open trunk again, then back. "What the fuck is he doing in your trunk, Smokey?" His voice tightened. "More importantly, why the fuck is he dead?"

"I don't know," Smokey said, blinking hard. "It all happened so fast. One minute I'm dropping off product, and the next... he's making moves on my girl."

Junior stared at him.

"Wait—" he held up a hand, trying to piece it together. "You took her to one of our drop-offs?"

"Yeah... I've done it before."

The girl sobbed softly, confused and frightened, knees pulled to her chest. Junior didn't even look at her—his focus was on Smokey, whose hands now shook, not from adrenaline, but realization.

Junior walked forward and grabbed Smokey's face with both hands, squeezing it as he stared dead into his eyes.

"You stupid motherfucker," he said quietly. "Do you have any idea what you could've brought down on us? What kind of heat?"

He let go, wiping his hands on his guayabera, turned and walked toward Flaco.

"Call El Carnicero." He said quietly, "Tell him we have three special cuts for delivery."

Flaco's eyes narrowed. He gave Junior a small nod and stepped away toward the stairs.

Junior looked to a couple of the soldiers hovering nearby. "Spread some plastic out on the floor."

He turned back to Smokey. "Hey. Help 'em pull that foo out the trunk. Apúrate."

Smokey hesitated, then obeyed, dragging the body with help from the two others. They laid it on the plastic like a package waiting for delivery. The girl hadn't moved.

Flaco reappeared and gave a signal.

Junior nodded. "Alright—listen up!" he shouted. "Everybody, go home. We're done for the day."

No one argued. The remaining soldiers cleared out. As Smokey moved to follow, Junior's voice cut through the air.

"Where the fuck you going, Smokey?"

"I thought—"

"What do you mean 'I thought'? Get your ass over here. I thought nada, pendejo."

Junior looked to Flaco. "Take the girl to my office. Wait there."

Flaco walked over, gently lifted the girl from the floor, and led her toward the stairs. She looked back once—eyes wide, body trembling.

Junior turned to Smokey, who was now standing alone in a warehouse that suddenly felt like a tomb.

He stood still for a moment, then walked slowly over to Smokey. No yelling. No threats. Just silence.

"You know what has to happen, right?"

Smokey's chin quivered. "Please, J—Junior… I didn't mean to…"

Junior raised his hand. "Don't talk. Go and kneel next to that foo."

He circled around him once, then stopped behind.

"You were never here."

One clean crack split the silence.

The body fell in stages—knees, then face, the life in his eyes—gone

Junior stood over the body, silent, the gunshots echo still hanging in the air like smoke.

He exhaled through his nose and holstered the pistol, then looked up toward the office window above. A shadow moved behind the glass. Flaco.

Junior made his way up the metal steps, each footfall sharp against steel. At the top, he pushed the office door open.

The girl was seated on the edge of the worn leather couch, hands clenched tight in her lap. Her eyes were puffy. Mascara smeared like ink stains down her cheeks. Flaco leaned against the far wall, arms crossed, watching her like a sentry.

She looked up when Junior entered but said nothing. She knew better than to ask.

He closed the door behind him. The room fell still. For a moment, he just stared at her, then dragged a chair across from hers and sat down.

"What's your name?" he asked, voice even, calm.

She hesitated. "Lexi."

"Lexi," he repeated, nodding slowly. "You from around here?"

She nodded. "Lynwood."

"You know who we are?"

Her eyes flicked to Flaco, then back to Junior. "Yes." She answered nervously.

Junior moved closer, his presence heavy but not aggressive. He wasn't trying to scare her. He didn't need to. The fear was already there, thick in the room like humidity.

"Lexi, I need to ask you something. And I need the truth. Not what you think I want to hear. Not what'll keep you alive a few more minutes. Just the truth."

She swallowed. "Okay."

"Did you see anything else at that drop?"

She blinked. "No. Just… the guy started flirting with me, I told him to stop and Smokey got mad. Next thing I knew, he hit him. And then—then he just kept going. He wouldn't stop. I tried to pull him off, but I couldn't."

Junior stared at her, weighing every word. She was young. Probably no older than twenty-two. Pretty in a rough-edged way. And now, caught in something she had no business being in.

He sighed and turned to Flaco. "Get her cleaned up. Give her some water. Then drive her home."

Flaco raised a brow. "You sure?"

"She didn't bring this. Smokey did."

Junior looked back at Lexi.

"You don't talk about tonight. Not to your girls, not to your mom, not to some dude trying to be cute over drinks. You keep this inside you like a sickness. Understand?"

Lexi nodded fast. "I swear. I won't say anything."

"Good. Because if you do." Junior didn't have to continue, she understood what he meant.

Junior opened the door and stepped out. Flaco followed after a beat.

"You're being merciful," Flaco said under his breath.

"Maybe I am." Junior kept walking toward the door. "Lexi, wait outside."

Lexi glanced at Junior, then at Flaco, before stepping out.

"Flaco—por las dudas—put one of your best on her. Keep eyes. If she even thinks about talking..."

Junior locked eyes with him. The rest didn't need saying.

"Simón, jefe," Flaco nodded.

The warehouse floor, was now being scrubbed down by two loyal hands in silence.

"Make that car disappear." Junior ordered

The crown didn't gleam like it did in the showroom. Not here. Not after blood.

It cut.

And it had to.

Flaco drove Lexi home, Junior got into his Mercedes and drove off.

El Carnicero pulled up in his Jeep. In the back: gallons of sulfuric acid.

A Thorn in the Crown

Junior stared out the passenger window, watching the scenery smear into a blur of scrubland, rusted fences, and roadside shrines. Every mile brought him closer to home, and further from the man he used to be.

He thought of everything that had brought him to this point.

Manny's voice still echoed in his head—calm, loyal, never asking for more than a straight word and a purpose. Junior had asked him for help, not knowing the weight it would carry. The trip to TJ to see Tico, sitting across from the man who once held the leash. The conversation was short, cold. No blessing. Just transfer of power.

Then came the fallout.

Manny's body. His blood. The funeral that didn't feel like one. The look in his mother's eyes that day, like she knew something had been lost for good.

And most recently—Lil Smokey.

Junior could still see him. Not the cocky, careless soldier he once was, but the shell that knelt before him. The panic, the stammering. The emptiness after the shot. The way his eyes turned glassy and lifeless. Not just dead—erased.

Junior shifted in his seat, jaw tightening.

It wasn't guilt exactly. Guilt was for those who could afford to look back. This was different. He was crossing a threshold now. There'd be no turning back.

This was the cost of the crown.

And it was cutting deeper every day.

The ring of his Nokia broke through the hum of the road and dragged him out of his thoughts. He reached into the center console and flipped it open.

"Hola, amá."

His voice softened. Whatever steel he carried in his day-to-day, it dulled the moment he heard his mother's voice.

"Mmhm... that's good to hear. And pops—how's he doing?"

He listened, eyes fixed on the road ahead though he wasn't really seeing it.

"Uhuh... okay. And what did the doctors say?"

A pause. Something in his jaw shifted.

"Mom, don't worry. I know he doesn't accept it, but money isn't a problem. I'll find him the best doctor. Whatever it takes to help with his recovery, okay?"

Another pause, shorter this time.

"Alright, mom. Love you too. Bye."

He closed the phone slowly and stared at it in his hand. Flaco said nothing from the driver's seat. He didn't have to.

The Suburban cruised along the empty highway, a dark vessel cutting through the last light of day. Golden streaks smeared the sky, giving way to deeper oranges and bruised purples. The road stretched ahead like a ribbon unraveling through desert and dust, its edges blurred by speed and heat shimmer.

Inside, silence ruled.

Junior leaned back, elbow resting against the door, fingers tapping slow against his knee. The hum of the tires was steady, hypnotic. Outside his window, power lines passed like the ticks of a clock, each one marking time he couldn't get back. Time before all this. Before the weight.

Flaco drove with both hands on the wheel, eyes forward, sunglasses still on despite the fading light. He hadn't said a word since the call ended.

Dust kicked up behind them, curling in spirals that caught the dying sun. They were a ghost—no music, no headlights, no witnesses. Just two men in motion, heading back to the warehouse, where the real world waited with blood under its nails and silence between every beat.

Junior exhaled slow, watching the sky darken. Whatever peace there was on this highway, it wouldn't follow them home.

The Suburban pulled up to the warehouse, streetlights casting a pale amber glow over the façade of the old brick building. The night air was still. Quiet.

Junior and Flaco made their way through the side door. Just inside, shielded from the elements by the roll-up bays, sat Junior's brand-new Mercedes S70 AMG—black on black, delivered earlier while they were still coming back from TJ. It gleamed under the overhead fluorescents, a phantom crouched low and still.

Flaco whistled low. "Oh snap! That shit looks hard, Jefe!"

Junior cracked a rare smile. A small reward for all the suffering he'd endured.

"It does look hard," he agreed, stepping around it slowly.

The body lines were smooth, elegant in the way only German engineering could deliver. The black-on-black scheme, the stance, the matching wheels—it gave the car the presence of a panther. Quiet, dangerous.

Junior opened the door. The scent of wood and Alcantara leather hit them instantly.

Inside, they explored the interior—buttons, dials, stitching that felt more like art than assembly. Everything in its place. Everything whispered power.

"Alright," Junior said, checking his watch. "Let's go. It's late. Let's meet up here tomorrow morning at six—we've got business to handle. My cousin's quince is coming up. I don't want anything getting in the way of that night."

Flaco nodded, then locked up and headed out.

Just as Junior was about to leave, a Crown Vic rolled up to the warehouse.

Benavidez.

Junior stepped out of the AMG and perched on the hood, arms resting on his knees, watching as the detective got out and approached.

"What's up?" Junior asked. "Something wrong?"

"Nope," Benavidez said. "But I heard you had a little problem."

Junior shrugged. "More like minute. Is that all you're here for?"

Benavidez stepped in a little closer. "Word on the street is there's a new crew trying to make moves. Some reckless young blood out of Vegas. Supposed ties to a new faction making noise down south."

"Yeah, I heard about that," Junior said, gaze flat. "News to me, though, about them wanting to make waves here in Bellavista."

Benavidez nodded slowly. "Listen—we went through one war already. And you and me..."

"I know." Junior looked him in the eye. Nothing else needed to be said. They both understood what could come. And what needed to be avoided.

"Just keep your eyes open," Benavidez said. "You're at the top of the totem pole now."

Junior stared off toward the dark, silent city. No response.

Benavidez turned and walked back toward his cruiser. As he opened the door, Junior called out.

"Benavidez—my cousin's quince is next Saturday. You're more than welcome to come through."

The detective paused, looked back with a faint smile, and nodded. Then he got in and drove off.

Junior remained for a moment, replaying the conversation. If something was coming to Bellavista, he'd be ready.

He slid into the driver's seat, started the engine, and Chalino came on the radio—his voice raw and righteous. Junior leaned back, the hum of the AMG wrapping around him like armor and drove off into the night.

The city rested beneath the weight of unknowing, while the winds turned bitter with omen. And he who wore the crown—though it cut—was all that stood between the people and the pit.

Thorns of the Throne

Vegas was prime territory for this business to thrive—an oasis of vice in the middle of the desert. Gambling, sex, greed… all legal, all loud. And beneath it all, a steady undercurrent of desperation. To the right mind, that made it the perfect feeding ground.

That's what Los Soldados de Querétaro saw early on.

A new faction. Newly blooded. Fresh off a violent split from a major cartel in central Mexico. They didn't ask for a seat at the table—they kicked it over, gunned down everyone sitting, and claimed the wood and blood for themselves.

Their methods weren't subtle.

Police chiefs woken at 2 a.m. by calls from burner phones. A quiet voice on the line: "We know who you are. We know where your family sleeps. If you don't back down, it won't be you we kill."

Duffle bags dumped in plazas with decapitated heads. Rivals hanging from bridges like broken ornaments. And yet—no innocent bystanders. That was their code. No stray bullets. No screaming mothers. Just targets. Just war.

They moved fast—ripping through former territories with precision, flooding corridors with product, forcing corrupt officials to either bend the knee or vanish. Vegas gave them a northern stronghold. But the real prize was expansion. And standing in their way were two choke points on the map:

Bellavista and La Sombra Negra.

Two names that echoed loud in the underworld. One a city carved from grit and loyalty. The other, a shadow empire with deep roots and deeper reach.

But Los Soldados weren't deterred. They had a weapon. A predator. A name whispered behind closed doors and border checkpoints:

El Puma.

No one knew his real name. Only the trail he left behind.

Not flashy. Not loud. He didn't posture or bark threats. He hunted. Waited. And struck when the prey was too comfortable to run.

Stories floated up from the south like dust storms. A house in Guanajuato where twenty men were found dead—no bullet holes, no blood. Just slashed throats, peeled faces. The only trace: a black puma painted in ash on the wall.

Another tale spoke of a crooked judge in Tijuana who ruled against a Soldado boss. The judge disappeared. Three days later, his body was found inside a nightclub freezer, curled into a fetal position, his eyes wide open and glassy. One claw mark carved across his chest.

No announcement. No manifesto. Just myth.

And now, that myth was heading north.

"El Puma wants Bellavista," someone whispered in a bar on the outskirts of Laughlin.

"El Puma's already here," another corrected. "He's watching."

A candle burned low in the back room of a panadería on East Charleston. The front served pan dulce and café de olla to unsuspecting locals. The back held secrets.

Concrete floors. One steel table. No windows.

Mateo "El Padre" Rocha sat at the head, smoke curling from a thick hand-rolled cigarillo clenched between his fingers. His guayabera was bone-white and crisp, unbuttoned just enough to show the gold scapular chain resting against his chest. His skin, weathered by years of sun and war, looked carved from stone.

Across from him, El Puma—silent, coiled—watched the candlelight dance across a set of folded maps laid out between them. The scent of tobacco, sweat, and warm bread hung in the air.

Rocha drew a circle around Bellavista with the black ink of a Montblanc.

"This city…" he muttered, voice deep and calm, "is not a stronghold. It's a checkpoint. That's all. Remove the checkpoint—move the line."

El Puma's head tilted slightly, like a predator sensing movement in the brush.

"¿Mandamos la señal?"

Rocha's eyes didn't leave the map. His lips curled, slow and deliberate.

"No. Not yet. First we whisper. Then we wait… to see who flinches."

He pressed his finger down over Bellavista.

"El norte no se toma por la fuerza. Se toma por el miedo de lo que viene."

El Puma said nothing. He didn't need to.

The whisper was already on its way.

Two days later, five members of Los Varrio Ghosts were found in an alley behind a laundromat—bound, gagged, and executed with precision.

Hands duct-taped. Mouths stuffed with cloth. Each shot once in the head.

No message left. No cartel tag.

Only a whisper drifting through the streets: El Puma had come to Bellavista.

Benavidez stood inside the warehouse, arms crossed, eyes locked on Junior.

"I don't like this," he muttered.

Junior didn't answer right away. He paced, jaw tight. "I don't like it either. You got nothing from your contacts? Informants?"

Benavidez shook his head. "Nada. Either they don't know shit, or they're too scared to say anything."

Junior stopped pacing. "Makes sense." He looked toward the far end of the warehouse, where the Suburban still carried dust from the border.

Then he made the call.

"I'm gonna hit up Tico," he said. "Have him send down Los Cuervos Negros."

Benavidez flinched. "What? Those motherfuckers again? Last time they were here, Bellavista turned into Juárez. People were scared out of their fuckin' minds."

"I know." Junior's voice was calm, but cold. "But we gotta hit this head-on. Or you're gonna have a bigger nightmare than me. At least we—" he gestured between them, "—have an agreement. Keep innocents out of it."

He paused. "These foos? From what I've heard? They ain't gonna be as nice."

Benavidez rubbed a hand down his face. "Jesus Christ…"

Junior's phone was already ringing.

Somewhere over the city, a black bird circled.

Not a crow. Not a vulture.

Something older. Meaner.

It didn't caw. It didn't cry.

It just watched.

And below, the streetlights of Bellavista flickered like candles at a funeral.

"Take and eat, says the altar; keep watch, answers the street."

—Book of the Saints, 9:11

Thorns at the Alter

Saturday had arrived faster than expected.

The sun pierced through the window shades of Junior's downtown apartment, casting long streaks across the wood floor. Dust danced in the light. He sat at the edge of the bed, bare feet planted, the silence holding him like a confession booth. The weight of the past few days—Lil Smokey, the whisper of El Puma, the call to Tico—sat heavy on his chest.

A new danger lurked just outside the frame of the day, but Junior knew: today wasn't for war. It was for his cousin.

He reached for the worn rosary that hung from the bedpost. His mother's. The one she used every night since Rafa's heart scare. The beads clicked softly between his fingers as he bowed his head. No words. Just breath, and the weight of a man asking for wisdom.

He crossed himself, eyes still closed.

Then rose, as if rising meant becoming someone stronger.

In the closet hung a suit that rarely saw the light—custom, tailored by a little Italian man downtown who dressed senators, sluggers, and the occasional dignitary. Deep navy, almost black, with hand-stitched lapels and a silken charcoal lining. A suit that said, I don't borrow respect. I wear it.

Junior ran his hand down the sleeve, then laid it carefully on the bed while he dressed. The shirt was crisp white. The tie, blood red. Every choice intentional. He tied the knot slow, methodical. Not vanity—ritual.

He slipped on his black Cayman Cuadra boots—polished, sharp, a silent nod to heritage and presence.

At the dresser, he clasped his gold Rolex around his wrist, its weight familiar, comforting in its permanence. He turned his hand slowly, inspecting it, as if it told time not in hours, but in decisions.

Then came the final touch. From a velvet-lined tray, he picked up a gold pinky ring, the obsidian stone at its center catching the morning light—black and ancient, like it held something inside. Maybe it did.

He slipped it on and looked in the mirror. Straightened his collar. Adjusted the tie.

No more loose ends. No more half-measures.

The man staring back at him wasn't the boy Rafa had raised. He was something forged. Hardened. Crowned by necessity, not desire.

After a light breakfast—eggs, toast, a black coffee that had long gone cold—Junior sat on the edge of the leather couch, listening to the morning news hum low from the TV. Nothing new. Just silence pretending to be peace.

Then came the chirp.

That sharp, unmistakable chirp of the Nextel.

Junior reached across the counter, picked it up, and answered flatly:

"Yeah."

Flaco's voice came through, low and casual. "I'm downstairs."

"On my way."

He slid the Nextel into his coat pocket, grabbed the Nokia from the entry table, and gave the apartment one last glance. A moment of stillness.

At the door, he paused.

He reached into his shirt and pulled out the rosary—his mother's. Pressed the cold crucifix to his lips, then to his forehead, chest, and shoulders. A silent plea for strength, maybe protection. Maybe just a habit too old to break.

He crossed himself once more. Then stepped into the hall and headed for the elevator.

"Buenos días, Señor Quintana. Looking sharp." Luis, the doorman said as Junior stepped out of the elevator.

Junior returned the nod and slipped him a folded twenty as Luis opened the glass lobby door.

"Gracias, carnal."

The sun outside was already climbing high, washing the streets in gold. The corner paleteros were out, their bells chiming in soft patterns, cutting through the hum of the 10 freeway nearby. Tires whispered against pavement, a constant rhythm that somehow made the city feel alive—less threatening.

Junior slid on his sunglasses. For a moment, the world darkened—then focused.

Across the driveway, Flaco stood beside the AMG, already holding the passenger door open like a chauffeur with street grit.

"Good morning, Jefe," he said, a slight grin breaking through the usual stone.

Junior gave a faint nod. "Good morning."

He stepped into the car, letting the scent of leather and polish wrap around him. Flaco circled to the driver's side and slipped in, hands steady on the wheel.

"Ready to head to the church?" Flaco asked. "Maribel should be pulling up soon in the limo. Your parents are already there, waiting on you."

Junior adjusted his cufflinks, gold catching the light. He looked out toward the city—his city—and nodded once.

"Let's go."

The Mercedes AMG eased to a stop just outside the plaza. The morning sun hit the cathedral's twin towers, casting long shadows over the ochre-colored stone. Junior stepped out, adjusting his jacket. Behind him, the fountain gurgled softly, and the distant clatter of shoes echoed off cobblestone.

He took in the sight of the Catedral de La Sagrada Corazón de Bellavista—she stood like a sentinel in the golden blaze of late morning, its twin towers reaching into the pale, sun-bleached sky. The yellow stone of the façade radiated heat, not just warmth, but that oppressive, unyielding kind that clung to skin and soaked into clothes. Even the plaza stones shimmered, the air above them bending with the days intensity.

At the base of the wide steps, a few early guests milled about in suits and pressed dresses. A child kicked a balloon near the iron fence, laughter echoing against the yellow municipal building next door.

Junior glanced up at the bells. For a moment, he remembered being a kid himself—running through plazas like this, never imagining one day he'd be standing here like this. A man with power. A man with enemies. A man with blood on his hands, dressed in a suit made for kings.

He adjusted his collar and ran a finger across his brow. Sweat—not nerves. He was used to nerves. This was something else. The kind of heat that made a man feel like he was being watched, like the sun itself was a spotlight and judgment loomed behind every darkened window.

To his left, a paletero wiped his forehead with a rag, ignoring the bells as they rang from the church above. A woman selling flowers fanned herself with a church bulletin. Life went on, but slower… more careful.

Junior stood at the top of the cathedral steps, one hand on the rosary in his pocket, the other close to the phone in his coat. The words from Benavidez still echoed in his ears like a whisper from fate.

Then came the low roll of the limo.

Heads turned. Cameras clicked. Someone in the crowd let out a low whistle.

The back door creaked open—and there she was.

Maribel stepped out like a star emerging from a dream, her gown catching the light in every direction. The deep navy fabric glistened under the sun's judgment, every golden embroidery glinting with flecks of fire. The gown swept around her in waves, adorned with ornate, gilded patterns that climbed like vines—baroque, elegant, commanding. But one cluster high on her side caught Junior's eye: a rosette stitched with such care, it mimicked the delicate, spotted geometry of a leopard's pelt.

Maribel's court fanned out behind her, laughing, posing for the photographers. Her tiara sparkled against the backdrop of sunbaked stone and distant church bells, and the crowd parted like waves to let her pass.

Junior scanned the rooftops, his eyes narrowing behind dark lenses. He took in every doorway, every shadow behind the yellow haze of light. Somewhere, someone could be watching—waiting. The silence between sounds was too thick, too knowing.

He stepped forward, crossing himself, his movements sharp. The great wooden doors of the church loomed before him.

And behind him, the heat whispered like a breath down his neck.

As the cathedral doors groaned open and Junior stepped into the cool shadows of the nave, something tugged at the edge of his vision. A sliver of movement across the sun-bleached street—a white Ford sedan, tucked halfway behind the corner of a taquería, engine idling low. Too clean. Too still.

He didn't stop walking, but his eyes slid sideways behind dark lenses. The glare from the windshield made it hard to see inside, but there was someone in there. Maybe two. The front passenger window was cracked, barely. No one got out. No one smoked. Just the steady thrum of an engine under heat.

Could've been nothing. Could've been paranoia. After all, he hadn't slept much, and the kind of weight he carried these days had a way of sharpening shadows into shapes.

Still, the hairs on the back of his neck lifted.

He made a slow sign of the cross and continued into the church, one step behind the swelling sound of organ chords. The heavy doors swung closed behind him with a dull boom, sealing the cool sanctity inside from the simmering world beyond.

But even with the incense thick in the air, even with the hush of ancient stone and candlelight, Junior couldn't shake it.

White sedan. Parked where it shouldn't be. Not moving. Not nothing.

He would remember.

The air inside the cathedral was cooler, but thick—an ancient stillness draped in incense and whispers, where the outside heat clung to the stone walls like memory. The moment Junior crossed the threshold, it felt like stepping into another world— one untouched by time, one still watched by angels.

Marble floors, polished to a mirror-like sheen, reflected the fractured light pouring through towering stained-glass windows. The colored panes danced in tones of crimson, sapphire, and gold, casting ghostlike hues across the aisle, made visible through the swirling tendrils of incense smoke and morning mist that filtered in through the high clerestory.

Heavy wooden pews, dark with age and reverence, stood in perfect order—lined like soldiers of faith. The lacquer had worn smooth from generations of hands gripping their edges during prayer, grief, and moments of quiet surrender.

Up ahead, flanking the altar, icons and statues loomed with solemn grace.

To the left, encased in soft votive glow, stood La Virgen de Guadalupe—her eyes tender and eternal, her robe a cascade of midnight blue and rose, rays of gold bursting behind her like the dawn of salvation. Candles flickered at her feet, each flame a whispered petition, each glass vessel clouded with soot and hope.

To the right, mounted above the transept arch, was San Miguel Arcángel, captured mid-battle. His wings, carved in mahogany and gilded at the tips, reached wide like judgment. His sword plunged through the breast of a coiled demon, his gaze unflinching—unyielding protector of the righteous.

And near the rear side chapel, surrounded by offerings of folded bills, rosaries, and photographs, was San Judas Tadeo. Patron saint of the hopeless. The desperate. The accused. His face wore the peace of one who had heard every plea imaginable—and never turned away. Behind him, graffiti-scarred candles burned beside hand-written notes scrawled on receipt paper and napkins.

The organ began to swell, its tones deep and cathedral-filling, vibrating through the arches like breath through lungs. It wasn't music. It was presence.

And for the first time that day, Junior felt something push back against the weight on his shoulders. Not relief. Not absolution.

Just the truth of something bigger than him.

Something watching.

As Maribel began her slow, radiant walk up the center aisle, flanked by her court of damas and chambelanes, the music softened and all eyes followed her. Junior watched with quiet pride, but his focus shifted as he scanned the crowd instinctively. His gaze caught a familiar figure near the front—his parents, seated just behind the velvet-rope pews reserved for padrinos and honored guests.

He moved toward them with measured steps, not wanting to interrupt the sacred flow of the ceremony, yet needing to be near them.

Before he could fully settle in, Father Santiago stepped away from the altar, his cassock flowing behind him like the slow turn of a tide. The priest approached with a warm but solemn expression, placing a hand gently on Junior's father's shoulder, then offering one to Junior.

No one heard what was said, but all could see the moment.

Heads turned. Whispers fluttered like incense smoke.

It wasn't gossip. It was respect.

Even in a house of God, even on a day meant to celebrate youth and tradition, power recognized power.

And the priest's reverence didn't diminish the sacred—it affirmed it.

Junior said little. Just nodded. But in his gut, the tension never left.

As Father Santiago leaned in, his words were quiet, for them alone. Junior nodded respectfully, catching only part of what was said. Something about God watching over the brave... and weighing the hearts of men in uncertain times.

It felt more like a warning than a blessing.

Junior's jaw tightened.

Not out of disrespect—but because the priest wasn't wrong.

He could feel it. In the air. In the way the candlelight flickered unnaturally. In the way even the marble seemed colder today.

Something was coming.

He turned slightly, scanning the congregation, noting faces, pairs of eyes that lingered too long, or not at all. He wasn't paranoid—he was prepared. The cost of leadership was constant awareness, and today he carried that weight in silence.

Then he looked back toward the altar—and toward Maribel.

For her, for his family, for all the quiet lives who depended on the peace he fought to protect… he would not waver.

The murmur of voices softened as Father Santiago stepped into view from the side of the altar, his vestments flowing with each slow, deliberate step. The gold trim of his stole caught glimmers of stained glass light as he approached the lectern. Behind him, incense still lingered, curling upward like whispered prayers toward the vaulted ceiling.

He looked out at the gathered families—mothers wiping tears discreetly, fathers in stiff suits pretending not to be moved, children fidgeting beside polished shoes. The church was full, but there was a reverent stillness that settled the room, as if the saints themselves had paused to listen.

With both hands resting on the wood, Father Santiago's voice rang out—gentle but firm, seasoned with the years.

"Brothers and sisters, we gather today in the house of our Lord to witness the sacred celebration of a young woman's journey into womanhood. A passage not just of age, but of spirit. Of grace. Of responsibility."

He paused to let the words land.

"In this life, God calls each of us to different paths. Some are meant to guide. Others to protect. And some... are meant to stand as both."

He turned, his eyes finding Junior in the pew.

"It is my honor now to welcome the padrino of this celebration, Señor Rafael Quintana Jr, who will bless us with a reading from the Holy Scriptures."

Heads turned as Junior stood.

The sound of his footsteps echoed as he approached the pulpit, each step heavy with the weight of expectation—and something deeper. The kind of weight that doesn't come from titles or money, but from the invisible yoke of a life lived between mercy and violence.

He looked out over the congregation—his mother with her hands folded, his father sitting straighter than usual, and Maribel, luminous in her dress, watching him with wide, adoring eyes.

Junior adjusted the mic and opened the leather-bound Bible to the marked page.

"A reading," he began, "from the Book of Psalms…"

His voice was steady, full of quiet conviction.

"Blessed be the Lord, my rock, who trains my hands for war, and my fingers for battle. He is my steadfast love and my fortress, my stronghold and my deliverer, my shield in whom I take refuge…"

Each word carried weight—far more than scripture. It was a confession. A calling. A promise. Junior's eyes did not waver from the text, but the meaning sat heavy in his chest.

"…who subdues peoples under me."

When he finished, he closed the book and stepped back. Not a sound in the room—just the rustle of a few breaths and the distant cry of a street vendor's bell outside the cathedral walls.

He returned to his seat.

His mother looked up at him with quiet pride.

His father did not move—but his eyes glistened.

Father Santiago returned to the lectern, his hands gently clasped before him.

"Gracias, Señor Quintana," he said, his voice warm. "A powerful reading. One that reminds us that God does not only call the gentle—but the strong. Those who protect, those who carry burdens unseen by others, they too are blessed in His eyes."

A few nods from the elders. Whispers of amén from the pews.

He looked out once more to the gathered families.

"And now, let us continue."

The service resumed—readings, hymns, the traditional blessings over the young woman before her court. But for Junior, the words began to wash over like static—familiar but far off, the way a radio plays in the background while thoughts take over.

He adjusted his cuffs, eyes lowering as his mind drifted again.

The white Ford sedan parked outside. Was it still there?

The word on the street about El Puma. Was it real, or just smoke?

Benavidez hadn't called back. That wasn't like him.

He could feel the weight of the rosary still in his pocket, the beads warm from earlier prayers. His jaw tensed slightly.

Stay present, he told himself. It's her day.

But business didn't wait. And neither did war.

His eyes scanned the stained glass windows, the shafts of holy light, the faces of saints who'd seen more suffering than any man could bear. He wondered what they'd say to him now. Would they absolve him? Warn him? Or simply stand in silent witness to what was coming?

Father Santiago raised the chalice and host with reverence, the light from the stained glass catching on the silver, casting soft hues of red and gold across the altar. The thurible swung slowly, tendrils of incense curling heavenward.

He stepped forward and addressed the congregation.

"Brothers and sisters, come forth now to receive the body of Christ."

A gentle murmur passed through the pews as the faithful began to rise. Junior remained seated, still lost in thought. The weight of a thousand moving pieces pressed down on him—El Puma, the white sedan, the Cuervos, Vegas, his people. War was a breath away.

A sudden pressure on his hand.

He looked down—his mother. Her small fingers squeezed his palm softly, grounding him.

Junior blinked, took a breath, and stood.

He filed into line with the others, moving down the center aisle beneath the eyes of saints in glass and stone. The sound of organ music filled the cathedral, solemn and holy, yet to Junior, it felt distant. Muffled. Like being underwater.

Every step forward brought a new echo—Manny's voice. Lil Smokey's lifeless eyes. The bound bodies of LVG soldiers. The silence of Rafa after the heart attack.

He swallowed hard. The rosary in his pocket felt like lead.

Then, he was there.

"The body of Christ?"

Father Santiago stood before him, wafer held aloft. The question hung between them for a moment too long.

Junior stared at the host.

He wasn't sure what to say. He wasn't sure he deserved it.

"Amen," he finally whispered.

The priest placed the wafer gently on Junior's tongue.

Junior crossed himself, bowed his head, and stepped aside. He made his way to the nearest pew, knelt slowly, and lowered his eyes.
And there, in the cool shadows of the cathedral, Junior prayed.

Not with eloquence. Not with the poise of a man at peace.

But with the desperate heart of someone who wanted to believe that even in the darkest hour, there was still something holy left to protect.

The final hymn echoed through the cathedral, the incense still lingering in the air like a veil. One by one, the congregation began to rise. Quiet murmurs and the shuffle of Sunday shoes on polished marble filled the space. Mothers gathered their children. Old men adjusted their hats. The weight of ceremony lifted as the people filed out of La Catedral del Sagrado Corazón de Bellavista, blinking into the harsh afternoon light.

Then came the sound of applause. Soft at first, then swelling like a wave.

Maribel emerged at the threshold with her court—lilac dresses swaying, heels carefully navigating the ancient stone steps. Her gown shimmered in the sun, each embroidered rosette catching the light like jeweled fire. For a fleeting second, the spotted stitching on the bodice looked almost feline—a predator's pattern camouflaged in beauty.

Photographers snapped their last shots. Aunties called her name, neighbors clapped, strangers smiled as if they knew her. The girls lined up and entered the waiting white limousine, its polished chrome gleaming like a blade beneath the sun.

From the top of the landing, Junior stood in the shade of the archway, eyes hidden behind dark lenses.

The white sedan was gone.

For now, everything appeared at peace. But his gut told him otherwise.

Footsteps approached behind him.

"Ready to head out?" Flaco asked.

Junior didn't answer right away. His gaze followed the limo as it pulled into traffic, then drifted toward the horizon.

"Yeah," he said finally. "But we need to make a stop first."

"From the father's wound the son drank a vow, and the night learned his name."

—Book of the Blood, 1:1

The Blood of the Son

Junior headed toward the AMG. Flaco followed.

"Where we headed?" Flaco asked, sliding into the passenger seat.

"To JC's," Junior replied. "He's got something ready for me."

Flaco was already around the car and into the driver's seat as Junior settled in. The engine growled to life, and the AMG pulled away from the church.

While Junior made his way across town, Maribel and her guests slowly arrived at the reception hall.

The venue was a Spanish-style villa built for nights like this—an oasis of light and joy tucked in the heart of Southeast L.A.

Whitewashed walls, terracotta roof tiles, and a porcelain fountain crowned with bronze cherubs marked the entrance. Through the open ten-foot double doors, an open-air courtyard unfolded: round tables draped in linens matching Maribel's dress, soft ribbon streamers above, and warm bulbs strung in lines like stars suspended in celebration.

The DJ was already spinning an '80s dance mix, warming the crowd, ushering in the night.

Across town, Junior and Flaco stepped into JC's workshop.

From the outside, it looked like any other building in Bellavista's industrial zone—no signage, no flair. But inside, it was something else: pristine, organized, reverent. Off to the side, a nickel and gold AK rested on a carpeted workbench, mid-assembly. Nearby, bluing tanks simmered, and firearms in varying states of completion lined the wall like a silent congregation.

A voice echoed from the back. "Be right there."

JC emerged from the washroom, wiping his hands on a towel, a stripped Beretta 92FS frame in one hand and the slide in the other. He grinned when he saw Junior.

"What's up, my boy," he said, slapping hands with him, setting the parts gently on the counter. He nodded toward Flaco. "What's up, Flaco? How's things?"

"All good in the hood, homie."

JC chuckled. "Right, right."

"JC, I'm here for that special order," Junior said.

"I got you." JC disappeared into the back and returned a moment later carrying a chocolate-brown leather briefcase. "It's all about presentation," he said with a smirk.

He placed the case on the counter.

For a second, all three men stood still—each aware of the weight of what was inside.

Back at the reception, the celebration had begun.

Laughter echoed beneath the ribbons. Women in heels and glittered dresses posed for pictures. Uncles clinked glasses, kids chased each other around the dance floor. Maribel took her place at the center table, radiant, beaming, surrounded by her court.

The music shifted. Cumbia now. The lights twinkled above like dusk stars.

And somewhere, Junior was getting dressed for war.

Back at the reception, the courtyard buzzed with life.

Guests fanned themselves with folded programs or napkins, laughing under the soft glow of hanging bulbs. The DJ, perched behind a faux-stone booth wrapped in pink and white silk, lowered the volume and leaned into the mic.

"A toda la raza que tiene hambre—ya llegó la comida! The best tacos in Southeast L.A.—Tacos El Gato! Get in line before they run out."

Cheers rippled through the crowd. Folding chairs scraped against tile as people stood, drawn to the scent drifting in from the far corner of the courtyard.

JC unlocked the briefcase and turned it toward Junior.

"Go ahead," he said. "Open it."

Junior slowly lifted the lid. His eyes widened.

Flaco's hand shot over his mouth.

"Oh shit, that's hard!" he blurted.

"Damn, JC… te aventaste, güey."

Inside the briefcase, nestled in black velvet, lay two Colt 1911 Government National Match pistols—chambered in .38 Super, plated in 24-karat gold.

Each grip was carved from ivory, the Sacred Heart of Jesus hand-painted with reverence and fire.

Junior reached in and lifted one of the pistols. He traced the edge of the slide with his thumb, reading the inscription out loud.

"Non timebo mala..."

JC nodded. "Psalm twenty-three. Means 'I will fear no evil.'"

Junior picked up the second pistol and turned it in his hand.

"Quoniam tu mecum es…"

JC smiled. "'For you are with me.' Figured it was fitting—one to carry, one to protect."

The taco stand stood beneath a string of lights, its banner hand-painted and bold: El Gato, with a grinning cartoon cat clutching a cleaver in one paw and a taco in the other. Smoke curled from the plancha like incense, curling slow and thin into the night air. Meat hissed. Cilantro was chopped with the rhythm of a street drummer.

From a distance, it all felt innocent—pure, even. But beneath it, something else lingered.

A predator hiding in plain sight.

Flaco checked his watch. "Junior, we gotta go."

"One last thing before you leave," JC said, reaching under the counter.

He set a plain paper bag on top and peeled it open. From inside, he lifted a brown leather double shoulder holster—smooth, aged hide with fine stitching and weight that meant quality. Under each arm: a molded cradle for his custom pistols and a double mag pouch. Embossed across each holster, rich and detailed, was La Virgen de Guadalupe—her eyes cast downward in sorrow, framed in rays of divine light. A guardian for a sinner.

Junior ran his fingers over the embossing, then slipped into the rig. He holstered each pistol, slid the spare magazines into their pouches, and rolled his shoulders once. The weight settled like armor. He pulled on his coat, the outline barely visible beneath the tailored fabric. For a moment, the tension in his chest loosened. The gnawing edge of paranoia dulled.

He wasn't just ready—he felt chosen.

"Vámonos, jefe," Flaco said, already turning for the door.

Junior looked back at JC. "You outdid yourself with these. Al rato te mando lo que te debo."

JC nodded with a grin. "No rush, my boy. Just handle business."

The music drifted back to full volume just as the DJ's voice faded. Platters clanged behind the folding tables, the smell of carne asada and cabeza now thick in the air. Tacos El Gato was serving from a food truck parked just past the open gate, the line already ten deep.

Rafa stepped out from the shade of a string-lit awning, scanning the crowd. He leaned toward his wife.

"¿Dónde está Junior?" he asked, eyes drifting to the dance floor, the fountain, the tables.

She shrugged without looking up. "No tarda en llegar. Ándale, ¿cuántos tacos quieres?"

"Tráeme dos de asada y dos de cabeza," he replied, still distracted.

On the far side of the courtyard, a group of kids darted past a display of brightly colored alebrijes—fantastical creatures brought in by one of the party planners for decoration. There were winged lizards, neon roosters, even a serpent with a crown of sunflowers. But off to the side, near a hedge wall away from the others, one stood alone.

A puma.

Sculpted with exaggerated fangs and swirling in deep reds, obsidian black, and flashes of gold, it crouched low, almost snarling. Not quite life-sized, but close. No placard. No spotlight. Just there—watching.

As the crowd moved, some guests passed it without noticing. Others gave it a quick glance before continuing toward the taco line or the drink station.

Minutes later, Junior stepped out of the AMG, coat buttoned, steps steady.

He passed the hedge wall, eyes scanning the venue, calculating the crowd—angles, exits, shadows. Then something caught his eye.

He paused. Turned.

The puma alebrije stared back at him.

Not with eyes, but with presence.

Junior studied it for just a beat too long before continuing past it, his gait unbroken. But something tightened behind his ribs. He didn't know why. He just felt it.

And somewhere deep in the brush of memory, the instinct whispered—

A hunter moves when no one's watching.

Junior stepped into the courtyard, and a wave of cheers rippled through the guests.

Heads turned, one after the other, drawn by the commotion near the back. At the court's table, Maribel stood on the balls of her feet. Her eyes widened the moment she spotted him. A smile bloomed across her face.

"Nino!"

She ran.

The crowd instinctively parted, letting her through. She threw her arms around him, unafraid of the weight he carried beneath his coat.

"This is the best quince ever!" she beamed.

Junior knelt slightly, his voice warm. "Yeah? The night's barely getting started. Just wait."

She grinned, gave him one last squeeze, and darted back toward her seat—her dress fluttering behind her like a monarch in flight.

Junior made his way through the courtyard, trading nods and half-smiles with familiar faces as the crowd parted for him. He moved with a quiet purpose—coat fitted just right, the weight beneath it known only to him. The gold of his chain flashed once beneath the lights as he passed the drink station.

Near the taco line, under a canopy of twinkling bulbs, he spotted them.

Rafa stood with a plate in hand, already digging into a taco, the edges of his mustache dusted with salsa roja. Next to him, Junior's mother stood like she always did—shoulders squared, hands busy, eyes everywhere.

As soon as she saw him, her whole face lit up.

"Mijo," she said, brushing off her hands on a napkin and moving toward him. "¿Ya comiste? ¿Quieres que te traiga algo?"

"I'm good, amá," Junior said, smiling softly. "You already ate?"

"He estado bien ocupada, cuidando que los demas esten bien." she replied, shaking her head with a half-smirk. "¿Pero que? ¿Te traigo unos taquitos de asada o de cabeza?"

Junior touched her arm gently. "Later. I promise."

She gave him a look—one of those maternal scans that saw everything, even the weight he tried to hide. But she nodded and returned to her spot by Rafa.

Rafa turned, wiping his mouth. "Mira nomás. You clean up nice."

"Had to represent," Junior said.

"You got your plate?" Rafa asked, motioning toward the taco stand.

"Not yet."

"Well, don't wait too long. They're going fast."

Junior chuckled and stepped closer, the three of them now standing together under the lights, for just a moment—whole.

Through the drinks and conversation, Junior never stopped scanning the courtyard. His eyes moved with ease, always watching.

LVG members were scattered across the dance floor and taco line—laughing, dancing, blending into the night like regular guests. But their presence was deliberate. Controlled.

Off in the far corner, Flaco leaned against a post like a silent sentinel, Modelo in hand, eyes sweeping the room without ever looking rushed.

Then Junior spotted him—Benavidez.

He gave a subtle nod and motioned toward the DJ booth. Benavidez got the signal and made his way over.

"You made it," Junior said.

"Of course," Benavidez replied, glancing around. "Ain't gonna pass up free food and booze."

Junior smirked.

"Can't stay long though, I'm on call."

"No worries. Go eat, drink. Enjoy yourself." Junior opened his arms, motioning to the party. "It's all on the house!"

Benavidez gave a slight grin, then turned back toward the crowd.

Junior watched him disappear into the stream of guests, then made his way back toward his parents' table. Along the way, hands reached out to shake his. Men nodded with respect. Women smiled as he passed.

Patrinus incarnate.

He moved like smoke through the crowd.

The sun had just dipped below the rooftops, leaving the courtyard bathed in amber string lights and the lingering warmth of summer dusk. Glasses clinked, laughter carried across tiled floors, and the scent of grilled meats still floated heavy in the air.

Then the DJ began to fade the music.

A hush swept over the crowd—not silence, but that anticipatory quiet that comes before something big. The DJ leaned into the mic with a grin that made half the front row start to whisper and nudge each other.

"Damas y caballeros… Ladies and gentlemen. Our gracious host has prepared a little surprise tonight. And I've been told," he said with a dramatic pause, "that this just so happens to be Maribel's favorite banda of all time."

The murmurs turned to gasps. Maribel and her court, mid-giggle, stopped. Her hands flew to her mouth.

"Coming all the way from Sinaloa… the number one banda in all of Mexico and California—¡Banda Jaguar de Sinaloa!"

The crowd erupted. Cheers bounced off the stucco walls. Folding chairs screeched as guests stood up to see. Trumpets blasted from the archway, bold and gold. Tubas grumbled with pride. The snare cracked like a pistol shot. Then came the melodic sound of the flutes, dancing above the thunder like birds over a battlefield.

From the far entrance, the members of Banda Jaguar marched in—black leather blazers, studded with glimmering rhinestones, boots gleaming under the courtyard lights, instruments already in motion. The courtyard transformed in seconds: guests swarmed to the dance floor, older couples clapping along, younger ones spinning in excitement. Someone screamed. Another wept. It was that kind of night.

At the edge of the chaos, the event photographer lifted his film camera to his eye. One click. Then another. The flash fired like lightning, freezing moments that would be pasted into photo albums and passed around for decades.

And as the music soared, as Maribel ran toward the stage with tears of joy sparkling in her lashes, somewhere behind the applause and motion, Junior stood still—watching everything. Taking it in. Measuring it all.

The king at the center of his kingdom.

But even kings can't outrun fate forever.

The banda played on—booming brass, thundering drums, and flutes dancing.

But to Junior, it all started to shift. The snare hits slowed. The bass from the tuba thumped like a heartbeat—his heartbeat. The crowd moved like tall grass in the savanna, heads and shoulders swaying in waves under the lights, each motion masking something deeper.

Rafa stood beside him, saying something about the music, about how beautiful the night turned out. Junior nodded, but the words didn't register. They were muffled, distant—like sound through thick glass.

His focus narrowed.

People danced in clusters, laughed, held drinks aloft. A girl tossed her hair back and spun into her cousin's arms. But in the gaps—those shifting pockets of space—movement. Subtle. Wrong.

Shadows.

A man with no drink. Another with hands in his pockets, not clapping. A third who hadn't touched a single taco. All moving, never fully stopping, faces half-lit, eyes never smiling.

Flaco, across the courtyard, his body was relaxed, but his head swiveled toward a commotion near the food line—a group of men getting loud over whose turn it was. Nothing out of place on paper. But it pulled his attention.

Junior clocked it all. His right hand instinctively touched the outline beneath his coat, fingertips brushing leather. La Virgen pressed against his ribs.

His breath slowed.

From the edges of the courtyard, something was drifting inward.

Not seen, but felt.

A pressure. A presence. Like the weight of eyes on the back of your neck just before something breaks.

The hunter was already inside the tall grass.

Rafa nudged him with a grin. "You see that guy drop his plate? Thought he was going to cry."

Junior nodded. "Yeah. I saw."

He hadn't.

Because every sense was stretching thin, reaching across the courtyard like a spider's web. And something—somewhere— was vibrating the thread.

He stayed by his father's side. Didn't move.

But in his mind, he mapped it all.

Exit through the alley behind the taco truck. That bench— good cover. DJ booth—bad angle. Flaco still across the way, but distracted. No eyes on the west gate.

The hunter was here.

He could feel it.

And the tall grass—the crowd, the noise, the joy—that's what made it so easy to hide.

A shadow pulled at Junior's attention—different from the rest.

It didn't drift with the music like the others. It moved toward him.

His eyes locked onto a pair across the crowd. Cold. Focused. Fixed on him. No sway, no smile, no confusion.

Junior's hand slid to the inside of his coat. Warm steel met his palm. His fingers curled around the 1911's grip.

He stood, body turning instinctively, shielding his father. Muscles tightened. The beat of the banda dulled. And then—

"¡Tío Rafa!" Maribel called out, twirling to the rhythm, cheeks flushed with joy.

She waved him over, laughter in her voice. "Come dance with me!"

Rafa chuckled, all heart and light, and rose to his feet.

In that moment—that single moment—he stepped into Junior's line of sight.

CRACK!

A single shot split the night air like a whip, sharp and unnatural, louder than the music, louder than breath.

Screams followed.

Maribel collapsed to her knees, hands over her ears. Plates crashed. Children cried. Women ducked behind chairs. Junior's mother threw herself toward the table's edge, her screams drowned beneath chaos.

Benavidez reached for his gun, shoulder bracing as he tried to push forward—but people, panicked and thrashing, slowed every step. Like wading through a wave of confusion.

Junior turned just in time to catch his father.

Rafa stumbled, confusion in his eyes, his hand clutching Junior's lapels.

"Mijo…" Rafa managed, breath catching in his throat. A dark thread of blood slipped from the corner of his mouth, staining the white of his guayabera.

Junior lowered him gently, knees buckling as he went down with him, holding him like a child holds something sacred that's breaking in their hands.

The world muted.

All sound gone, swallowed in a vacuum of shock.

The gold-plated 1911 now rested in Junior's hand—unfired. The other hand clutched Rafa's shirt, blood soaking through the fabric.

Benavidez broke through the crowd just as Rafa's head tilted back, eyes losing their focus.

He was too late.

Junior didn't look up.

Didn't speak.

His chest heaved. Muscles locked. Veins bulged.

And then—from some ancient, buried place inside him—a guttural scream erupted, not in fury, but in grief too heavy for silence. It struck the air like a thunderclap, commanding stillness from the living and the dead alike.

Not words. Not rage. Grief. Pure and raw, clawing its way out from the depths of his soul. It silenced the night. Froze the dancers. Paralyzed the guests.

Then—stillness.

All the air left his lungs.

Silence. The kind that comes after the world changes forever.

People stared.

Some backed away slowly. Others watched, frozen in place.

Junior, still gripping his father's body, eyes wild, jaw clenched, was no longer the padrino.

He was a son cradling a broken world.

Flaco pushed his way through the crowd, eyes locked on Junior.

Benavidez, stalled for half a second, shock burning off fast. He snatched his radio and keyed in.

"David Sam 3," he barked. "Shots fired at a private venue— civilian down. Repeat: shots fired, likely DOA. I need units rolling code 3 now — lock down this whole block."

The radio crackled back, barely cutting through the thick, broken silence.

Maribel sat collapsed on her knees, sobbing uncontrollably, her makeup streaked down her cheeks like war paint.

Junior's mother knelt beside Rafa, cradling his head in her lap, rocking gently, whispering his name through tears. "Mi amor… mi amor…"

Junior stood motionless, the golden Colt .38 Super limp at his side, his suit dusted in the spray of shattered celebration. His eyes were scanning but empty—like a hunter with no more targets, only ghosts.

Somewhere in the distance, sirens began to wail—low at first, but growing louder, weaving through the city like a wolf pack closing in.

The lights above still twinkled, the music long silenced, yet the beat of that tuba still pulsed in the memory of the moment—like a phantom heartbeat that wouldn't stop.

The sirens drew closer, but in Junior's ears, there was only silence.

Not even his father's fading breath could break through it. Not the sobs. Not the shouts. Just that silence—thick, absolute.

And in that silence… something ancient stirred.

Something older than law, than blood, than the codes men pretend to live by. It wasn't born of vengeance—it was forged in the space between love and loss, where mercy doesn't survive.

A force woke in Junior that night—not one that could be seen or named but known. Felt.

And though no one in that courtyard understood what they had witnessed, the underworld would come to know it by many names:

Some would call it El Silencio.

Others, El Hijo del Dolor.

But all would come to fear what rose from Rafa's final breath.

The boy died that night.

What stood in his place…

It was the blood of the son.

"And I looked, and behold a pale horse: and his name that sat upon him was Death, and Hell followed with him."

—Revelation 6:8

About the Author

Lopez is a multidisciplinary creator whose work blends with gritty realism, philosophical undertones, and raw emotion. Being an entrepreneur, gunsmith, leather craftsman and writer, his storytelling spans fiction, design, and social commentary.

He is the founder of Veiled Truths Press and when not writing, you can find him customizing firearms, making leather goods, or working in his Southern California workshop.

Connect with him:

www.thelopezbooks.com

@kingdom05

Kingmagot.substack.com

Also by Lopez

Veiled Truths: The Lucian Graves Mysteries Vol's 1-3

A trilogy exploring secrets, survival, and the cost of clarity.

Interim

A haunting blend of noir and psychological suspense.

The Witnesses: The Fall of Eden

A cosmic reckoning that challenges the fate of humanity.

Find them at www.thelopezbooks.com

9 798993 735900